"Brad…" She ra[_____] up at him. She w[_____] she intended to say. But his face was intimately close to hers and his eyes held a flame that half stole her breath away.

"Simone," he whispered softly.

She knew if she leaned into him, he would kiss her…and she would kiss him back. And then she would want more…and more from him. Instead of leaning into him, she jumped up from the sofa. "I…I think it's time for me to head to bed. I'm completely exhausted."

He cleared his throat and stood as well. "The storm seems to have passed, so you should sleep well."

"Then I'll just say thank-you and good night." She went into the bedroom, sank down on the edge of the bed and drew a couple of deep breaths. The storm outside might be over, but a storm inside her continued to rage on.

* * *

Colton 911: Chicago—Love and danger come alive in the Windy City…

* * *

If you're on Twitter, tell us what you think of Harlequin Romantic Suspense! #harlequinromsuspense

Dear Reader,

I have a special place in my heart for the Colton books, having written one of the very first books that introduced the Colton family to readers. Just when I think there are no more Coltons left in the world, another branch pops up that is just as exciting, just as dramatic as the last.

I love this family, who have strong moral values and a real love for each other. They may have their issues with each other, but their love is always present. They argue, they fuss and they also laugh a lot together.

Heck, on most days I wish I was a member of this amazing family. I want to be a Colton!

Hope you all enjoy my story!

Carla Cassidy

COLTON 911: GUARDIAN IN THE STORM

Carla Cassidy

HARLEQUIN

ROMANTIC
SUSPENSE

Special thanks and acknowledgment are given to Carla Cassidy for her contribution to the Colton 911: Chicago miniseries.

Recycling programs for this product may not exist in your area.

ISBN-13: 978-1-335-62897-8

Colton 911: Guardian in the Storm

Copyright © 2021 by Harlequin Books S.A.

This edition published by arrangement with Harlequin Books S.A.

For questions and comments about the quality of this book, please contact us at CustomerService@Harlequin.com.

Harlequin Enterprises ULC
22 Adelaide St. West, 40th Floor
Toronto, Ontario M5H 4E3, Canada
www.Harlequin.com

Printed in U.S.A.

Carla Cassidy is an award-winning, *New York Times* bestselling author who has written over 170 books, including 150 for Harlequin. She has won the Centennial Award from Romance Writers of America. Most recently she won the 2019 Write Touch Readers Award for her Harlequin Intrigue title *Desperate Strangers*. Carla believes the only thing better than curling up with a good book is sitting down at the computer with a good story to write.

Books by Carla Cassidy

Harlequin Romantic Suspense

Colton 911: Chicago

Colton 911: Guardian in the Storm

The Cowboys of Holiday Ranch

A Real Cowboy
Cowboy of Interest
Cowboy Under Fire
Cowboy at Arms
Operation Cowboy Daddy
Killer Cowboy
Sheltered by the Cowboy
Guardian Cowboy
Cowboy Defender
Cowboy's Vow to Protect
The Cowboy's Targeted Bride

Colton 911

Colton 911: Target in Jeopardy

Visit the Author Profile page at Harlequin.com for more titles.

For my father, who taught me everything I needed to know about laughter and love. I will love you forever, Daddy!

Chapter 1

Simone Colton walked out of the large brick building that housed the psychology department on the University of Chicago campus. As she stepped into the sunshine, she drew a deep breath of the fresh early June air.

She should be feeling a big sense of relief. Today had been the last of the psychology classes she taught during the day. She had only a couple of night lectures left and then she'd be completely finished with the semester.

She had decided not to teach summer school and so she had two months of free time. Under normal circumstances she would have been looking forward to lunches with good friends, long naps and reading for pleasure and not research.

However, these were not normal circumstances. Nothing had been anywhere near normal since her father and her uncle had been brutally murdered, gunned down in the parking lot outside Colton Connections, their very successful family business.

The murder had occurred six months ago, and since that time, not only had Simone dealt with a mountain of grief, but also with the burning need to create a profile for the killer.

Right now, she was on her way home to change clothes and then she was meeting her sister Tatum at her restaurant. She needed to hash over the family meeting they'd had the night before with FBI agents Brad Howard and Russ Dodd, a meeting that had only renewed her burning need to catch a killer.

It was a short walk from the college campus to her condo in Hyde Park. She'd loved the condo the first time she'd looked at it and had considered it a lucky score in an area that was highly desirable.

However, since the murder, there had been no solace within the walls she called home. All she thought about was that her father would never be able to walk through the door again. He would never stop by to share a cup of coffee again. He would never, ever again be able to give her the big bear hugs that she'd loved, that she'd always counted on from him.

She now walked through the front door and tossed her briefcase on the overstuffed beige sofa that was bedecked with throw pillows in the color of soft pink magnolia. The same colored blinds hung at her floor-to-ceiling windows. The colors had once created a warm and soothing ambience, but nothing soothed her since her father's death.

The kitchen was updated with granite counter-tops and stainless-steel appliances, although she wasn't much into cooking.

The condo had two bedrooms and she now walked into the smaller of the two. This was her home office, where she graded students' papers and made up her lesson plans. Right now, the white-board that hung on the wall held notes that had nothing to do with her classes.

All the notes were on deviant personalities and behaviors, five months of her work in an effort to come up with a profile of her father and uncle's killer.

Despite her best efforts, she couldn't have been more wrong about things. It was time...past time for her to clear the whiteboard. She grabbed her eraser and slowly erased the notes she'd worked on so feverishly since the night of the murder up until a couple of weeks ago.

When she was finished, her heart clenched as she stared at the board of nothing that was left. It had been that easy for two thrill-seeking kids to erase her father from her life forever. Her grief was still like a clawing, vicious animal inside her that refused to relinquish its hold on her.

She whirled out of the office and went into her bedroom before the tears that were always close to the surface broke loose. It took her only minutes to change from the casual clothes she'd worn for class that day into black slacks and a dressier blouse. She always dressed up when she went to her sister's restaurant.

Minutes later she was on the train and headed downtown. As the train moved down the tracks, she leaned her head back and released a weary sigh. Since the murder, she'd been suffering from nightmares, haunting and horrible dreams where her father begged her to find the killers and seek justice for him and his brother. The nightmares didn't occur every night, but they did happen often enough that she sometimes felt like she was moving through life in a bit of a fog.

Seventeen minutes later the train halted at the stop closest to her sister's acclaimed restaurant. The restaurant, True, had opened two years ago to critical acclaim and commercial success.

Tatum had her dream come true with the restaurant and now she had the love of her life in the handsome Cruz Medina. Cruz was a Chicago cop who had gone undercover in the restaurant to investigate a potential drug ring working out of True.

By the time the case wrapped up, the two had fallen in love.

Simone now walked through the front door of True. Wonderful scents immediately assailed her nose. Even though it was late for lunch and early for dinner, the place was still packed with diners.

Before the hostess could greet Simone, Tatum approached with a smile on her face. Simone could always tell what her sister was doing in the restaurant that day by her hairstyle. If her blond hair was down and wavy, then Tatum was working front of the house. If it was a day when she was cooking, her hair was pulled back and up. Today it was down and she was clad in navy blue slacks and a blue floral blouse that emphasized her bright blue eyes.

"Come on, sis, I've got a two-top table in the back just waiting for us."

"Sounds perfect," Simone replied. She followed her sister through the stylish main dining room, where there was a large marble bar with tons of seating. Located in a warehouse, the restaurant boasted high ceilings painted green and huge windows that provided lots of natural light.

The space was decorated with a touch of a European bent, and the food was fresh farm to table. They went to the back and into a more private and quiet area. The minute the two were seated, a waitress with the name tag Annabelle appeared.

"Why don't you start us off with two glasses of white wine," Tatum said. "Thank you, Annabelle."

Minutes later the two had their wine and had ordered their lunch. "How are you doing?" Tatum asked.

Simone shrugged. "Still working through the grief."

Tatum nodded. "Aren't we all."

"It's somehow more difficult to get past knowing that there was absolutely no motive, that they were killed by two teenagers because they were in the wrong place at the wrong time," Simone said. "And then the killers went on to kill two more men, also with no motive whatsoever." A new wave of grief swept over Simone.

"I know, but thanks to Allie Chandler at least now they have one of the teenagers behind bars and they know who the other one is," Tatum replied.

Allie Chandler was a private investigator hired by their cousin Jones Colton. She was the one who had found social media posts from both of the boys. Jared Garner and Leo Styler had each written "score" on the nights of the murders.

"Thank goodness Allie wasn't hurt when they basically kidnapped her." Tatum took a sip of her wine.

Allie had gone undercover as a college student in an effort to get hard evidence that the two were responsible. She'd gotten herself invited to a party, but then the two boys had taken off with her in their car and ended up in Leo's parents' basement. When they'd discovered she was wired, the two teens had gone wild. Thankfully the FBI had broken in. Jared was arrested, but Leo had gotten away.

"I can't believe right now the only charge Jared is facing is kidnapping when we're all certain he killed Dad and Uncle Ernest," Simone said, her frustration evident in her tone.

"Unfortunately, Jared's and Leo's parents alibied them for the time of the murder."

"Yeah, their very wealthy, privileged parents and we have some proof that they were probably lying. Let's just hope the FBI can find Leo before his mommy and daddy can get him a ticket out of the country," Simone said.

The conversation was interrupted by the return of Annabelle with their meals. Everything that came out of the True kitchen not only had tremendous flavors but also beautiful presentations. Even the house salads that both of them had ordered looked like colorful works of art.

"Did you get the text from Heath about the family meeting tonight?" Tatum asked as soon as Annabelle had left their table.

"Yes, do you know what it's about?" Simone speared a cherry tomato with her fork.

"I don't have a clue."

Simone frowned thoughtfully. Heath was their eldest cousin and had temporarily stepped into the position of president of Colton Connections after the murder had occurred. "I just can't imagine what he would have to discuss with us. I'm assuming everything is going well at the business."

"I guess we'll find out tonight," Tatum replied.

For the next few minutes, the two ate and talked about their work and how other family members were doing. There were six cousins all around the same age and they were a very close-knit group.

"So, what are your plans for the summer?" Tatum asked when they were almost finished with their meals.

"I want to find Leo Styler and prove that those two little creeps are cold-blooded killers," Simone said fervently.

"Oh, Simone, please leave it all up to the FBI now," Tatum said, a troubled look on her face. "The last thing any of us would want is to lose somebody else."

"Don't worry. I'm not going to get myself into any kind of trouble," Simone replied. "However, I do intend to talk to Agent Howard and see if I can sit in on one of their interviews with Jared."

"He's not going to allow that. He seems to be a by-the-books kind of agent."

"His by-the-books style didn't catch the bad guys. A private investigator did." Simone shoved her plate aside and reached for her wineglass.

"That's not fair," Tatum said softly.

Simone released a deep sigh. "I know. I'm just sick of all the red tape and regulations. Besides, you know I'm always interested in what drives deviant behavior. I just want to learn more about Jared Garner and what drove him and his friend to commit such a terrible crime."

"You seem very intense whenever Agent Howard is around." Tatum arched an eyebrow and smiled. "I thought maybe something else was going on."

Simone looked at her sister blankly. "Like what?"

"Like maybe a little bit of attraction?"

"Don't be ridiculous," Simone scoffed even as she felt a rise of heat fill her cheeks. She wouldn't want anyone to know just how hot she found FBI agent Brad Howard.

His dark brown hair was worn short and neat and his hazel eyes appeared to change colors depending on what color of shirt he wore. He was tall with broad shoulders and an athletic build. She definitely found him more than a little bit attractive.

"I don't even like him very much," she told her sister. "I feel like I've dated versions of him in the past. He strikes me as being very stubborn and far too confident in himself. He probably finds it difficult to listen to anyone's advice and would never consider a woman his equal," Simone finished.

Tatum stared at Simone as if her head had just dropped off her shoulders and rolled across the floor. "That certainly hasn't been my impression of Agent Howard. I think maybe you're projecting shades of Dr. Wayne Jamison on him."

"Ugh, don't remind me of him." Wayne was a history professor at the college. She had dated him for a little over six months and had made herself believe she was madly in love with him. But the longer they had dated, the more controlling and superior he'd become. She'd finally realized he wasn't the man for her and so a year ago she'd broken things off with him. She hadn't dated anyone since then.

And the last thing she wanted from Brad Howard was any kind of a personal relationship. All she wanted was for him to alow her access to sit in on Jared Garner's interview. She might be able to help him put away two teenage serial killers.

FBI agent Brad Howard was frustrated. He'd been frustrated for the past two months, ever since he'd been called to Chicago from his Washington, DC, office to investigate the potential of two serial killers in the early stages of their "careers."

He now sat in the small office he'd been moved to a week ago. It was little more than a closet, but the Chicago PD had needed back the space he'd originally been assigned.

It didn't matter to him what kind of room he worked from. All he really needed was a desk, his phone and his work computer. Finally, they'd gotten the break they'd needed to identify two potential suspects. One was in jail and the other one wasn't, which created a lot of Brad's frustration.

He had spent much of his first month here assuming they were looking for a single killer. Serial killers working in duos certainly weren't unheard of, but they were relatively rare. One of the most famous killing duos was probably cousins Kenneth Bianchi and Angelo Buono Jr.

Together they had kidnapped and strangled ten women and girls, earning them the name of the Hillside Strangler in the press.

However, it was almost unheard of to have a couple of teenagers on a path of death. Jared Garner and Leo Styler were only nineteen years old. They both came from affluent backgrounds and right now Brad's biggest enemies were their parents, who were not being cooperative in the investigation. Rather, they were overbearing and overly protective people who used their money and their power to try to intimidate.

He now powered down his computer with thoughts of dinner on his mind. He'd been eating so much fast food and sandwiches in the past two months he'd decided that this evening he'd treat himself and go to a restaurant and have a real, good sit-down meal. However, before he could get away, an officer stepped into the room.

"Simone Colton is here to speak to you. Do you have a minute for her before you head out?" he asked.

"Of course. Send her on back," Brad replied. He braced himself for seeing her one-on-one. There was something about Simone that somehow unsettled him. More than any of the other family members, her grief haunted him and her intelligence challenged him.

He hadn't realized just how small his new office was until she was seated in a chair in front of his desk. Instantly he was engulfed by the smell of her perfume…an appealing scent of fresh flowers and a hint of fresh citrus.

"What can I do for you this afternoon, Miss Colton?" he asked.

"I've told you before you can call me Simone," she replied. Her eyes appeared a startling blue today. Her medium brown hair curved around her chin, emphasizing her delicate features. She was clad in black slacks and a tailored black-and-white blouse that showcased her slender shapeliness. "I was wondering if it would be possible for me to sit in the next time you interview Jared Garner."

He stared at her in disbelief as he shook his head. "You know I can't allow you to do that."

"Why not? I promise you I would be completely professional." She sat up straighter in the chair.

"That's not the issue. You're the victim's daughter, and in any case, it's against regulations." He could tell his words irritated her.

"I've spent all of my adult life studying the human mind and deviant behavior. I feel like I could help. Maybe I can see things in Jared that nobody else has seen…something that could help to get him to confess to the murders and give up Leo Styler's location." She leaned forward, her eyes burning with intensity. "I can help, Agent Howard. Please let me help."

He understood her desire…her absolute need to see that her father's killers were arrested and went to prison. He'd worked with enough victims in his career to know where she was coming from, but there was no way in hell he could or would allow her into an interview room with a suspect. It would certainly give a defense lawyer plenty of ammunition to use and there was no way Brad would risk the case they were building against the teens.

"I'm sorry, Simone. It just isn't allowed," he finally said. He watched as the flame in her eyes dimmed and instead a bleak despair darkened them. His chest tightened with sympathy.

"I still believe I might be able to pick up on things that everyone else has missed. I've been studying people and their behaviors for years," she repeated and then stood.

"Wait," he replied and frowned thoughtfully. An idea blossomed in his head, an idea that might give

Simone what she wanted and still keep the integrity of the investigation.

She sank back down in the chair and looked at him hopefully. God, she was so attractive. There was something about her that drew him in a very unprofessional way and that was the last thing he needed or wanted.

"I suppose if you want to come in tomorrow morning around ten, I could share with you the interviews we've already done with Garner," he offered.

Immediately her eyes brightened. "Oh, thank you. That would be wonderful. Then I'll see you at ten tomorrow." She jumped out of her chair, murmured a goodbye and then practically ran from the room as if afraid he might change his mind.

Even though he could think of all kinds of reasons why what he'd just offered her was probably a bad idea, he only hoped it helped in some way to ease her grief and come to terms with her uncle and father's murders.

Yes, for some inexplicable reason Simone's grief hit him much harder than any of the other Colton family members'. It was her sad eyes that haunted his dreams, her tears that had pushed him to try harder.

If he was perfectly honest with himself, he'd admit that the reason he'd just made the concession to allow her to see some of the interview recordings was because he'd pretty much failed her. He'd failed them all.

He'd worked dozens of serial killer cases in the past. In each case he had successfully worked up accurate profiles that had led to arrests in almost all of them.

In the past two months he'd done what he'd always done…tried to profile the kind of person the killer might be. Then two weeks before, a private investigator had shone a light on two nineteen-year-old college kids, proving that all of Brad's theories about the killer had been wrong.

He was now even more determined to prove that Jared Garner and Leo Styler had not only murdered Ernest and Alfred Colton in cold blood, but two other older businessmen as well. More than anything, he wanted to prove himself to all the Coltons, but particularly to Simone.

And that worried him. The last thing he wanted was any kind of tangled relationship with a member of the victims' family. Besides, hopefully it was now just a matter of days before they got Leo Styler behind bars and the case would be closed.

And it was probably just a matter of days before he would be back home in DC. After two months of living in a hotel and being immersed in murder, he should be looking forward to getting back to his life in DC. It worried him just a little bit that he wasn't.

When the case was over, he wouldn't mind hanging out here in Chicago for a little while longer. When he tried to identify why he would want to remain, it worried him that Simone Colton's beautiful face filled his mind.

There was no way he was going there. He was thirty-six years old and married to his work. Besides, no matter how attractive he found Simone Colton, he knew he would probably always remind her of one of the very worst times in her life.

Chapter 2

Heath had gathered the family together in Simone's mother and father's home. Her uncle Ernest and aunt Fallon's and Simone's parents' homes shared a common backyard with a large pool, pool house and tennis courts.

Although her aunt and uncle's place was exquisitely decorated in a French provincial style, it was somehow colder…less inviting than Alfred and Farrah's warm, Tuscan-feel home. Therefore, this was the place always chosen for family gatherings. Besides, with a mother-in-law suite attached, it made it easy for Grandma Colton, who lived in the suite, to be included in all the gatherings.

They were all seated on the overstuffed sofas

and on chairs brought in so everyone had a place to sit. Simone was grateful to sit on the sofa next to her mother.

Her aunt Fallon and her mother were twins. The main way people told them apart was that Farrah's dark brown hair was worn short and curly and Fallon's hair was longer. Simone's mother had always been the louder of the two. She was wonderfully loving and was the creative force in Gemini Designs, an interior design company she had started and now operated with her twin sister.

Since the murder, the spark in her mother was gone and her beautiful green eyes often held the same sadness, the same grief that Simone felt. It hurt Simone to see both her mother and her aunt trying to deal with the unexpected deaths of their husbands.

"I'm sure you're all wondering why I got you together this evening," Heath said and stood from his chair. Her cousin's dark blond hair was shaggier than usual and it was obvious he'd forgotten about shaving again.

Heath had stepped in as the president of Colton Connections, the company started by Ernest and Alfred and that was now valued at over sixty million dollars. The two men had created a series of innovative inventions and owned numerous patents.

"I'm sure wondering why we're all here," Grandma Colton replied.

Everyone looked at Heath expectantly. He drew in a deep breath. "Uh, something unexpected has come up concerning Colton Connections."

What now? Simone reached out and took her mother's hand in hers. Her mother squeezed her hand tightly, as if expecting bad news.

"My office has received a letter saying that half of Colton Connections's holdings rightfully belong to two other men. They are twins Erik and Axel Colton and they are claiming to be the illegitimate children of Dean Colton."

Gasps of surprise filled the room, along with exclamations of disbelief. Simone's stomach sank. Illegitimate children of her grandfather? Was this somehow true? Or were these two men simply vultures who were trying to capitalize on a double murder? As if they all didn't have enough to deal with already, and now this?

Heath raised his hands to quiet everyone. "They claim to be rightful heirs because of a special codicil Grandpa Dean drew up and they are therefore due the same amount of money that went to my dad and Uncle Alfred."

"I certainly never heard Alfred talk about having two illegitimate brothers," Simone's mother said.

"Same with me," Aunt Fallon added. "Ernest never mentioned having other brothers and I can't imagine Dean having an affair. But then before six months ago I wouldn't have imagined that my husband and his twin brother would be murdered."

There was a long moment of silence. "So, how serious are we taking this?" Simone's youngest sister, January, asked, breaking the hushed quiet that had momentarily overtaken everyone. January was a social worker for the county and volunteered for multiple organizations.

"Serious enough that I've gotten our lawyers involved. I just wanted to let you all know what was going on," Heath said. "And I'll continue to keep you all up to date as this whole thing unfolds."

A half an hour later Simone and her sisters left the house. "Oh, by the way, tomorrow I'm going to watch the files of the interviews of Jared Garner with Agent Howard," she told Tatum.

"You actually got him to agree with that?" Tatum asked in surprise.

"Wait…what's going on?" January asked. At twenty-seven years old, she was five years younger than Simone. January looked even younger than her age and was model pretty, so she was often not taken seriously, but Simone knew her baby sister was smart as a whip.

She quickly explained to January what she was doing the next day, and when she was finished, concern shone from January's green eyes. "Oh, Simone, I wish you would leave this all alone and let law enforcement do their jobs."

"That's exactly what I told her earlier today when we had lunch," Tatum said.

"I am letting them do their jobs," Simone protested. "I'm just hoping to help a little bit. I need to do this."

"I know how badly you're hurting, Simone. We're all hurting, but I don't want you anywhere near Jared Garner. Have you forgotten that Leo Styler is still on the loose? I don't want you getting any attention that might put you at risk," January exclaimed.

"My feelings exactly," Tatum chimed in.

"Don't worry. I'm just going to be in a little office with Brad Howard and nobody will even know I'm there. Trust me, I'll be fine." Simone hugged January and then Tatum.

"What do you think about what we just heard from Heath?" Tatum asked.

"I find it darned suspicious that after all these years and only after Dad and Uncle Ernest are gone, these twins magically appear out of the blue," January said.

"I agree, but I also trust Heath and the attorneys to sort it all out," Simone replied. "And on that note, I'm heading home." She hugged each of her sisters once again and then got into her car and headed back to her condo.

Once there she found it impossible to think about what had just happened when her head was so full of what she hoped would happen the next day. She desperately hoped she'd see something on the file that could be used to break Jared into confessing to the murders.

She changed out of her clothes and into a sleeveless summer nightgown. After washing her face and brushing her teeth, she finally climbed into her king-size bed. She'd bought the bed when she'd thought she was going to have a future with Dr. Wayne. He'd lived in a cramped apartment and so they had spent most of their time together here in her place.

But she had refused to let him move in with her and she also didn't like him spending the night with her. In her mind that was something engaged or married couples did.

She'd finally kicked out the doctor but had kept the bed. There were times she felt very lonely. At thirty-two years old she had the career of her dreams, but she was missing the dream man in her life.

Eventually she wanted a big family and she'd begun to hear the faint tick of her biological clock. Still, she wanted to be married only once and so it was important she get it right the first time.

She fell asleep almost immediately and into the dream that far too often haunted her nightscapes. She was in a graveyard and walking along a dark path between the headstones. The moonlight was full and cast down a haunting silvery light. Her heart clenched as she came to the headstone where her father's name was written.

In her dream she sank down to her knees before it, tears half blinding her. "Daddy, I miss you so much. You've always been my hero and now I'm absolutely lost without you."

A mist began to form across the front of the headstone, a mist that came together and became her father's beloved face. "Help me, Simone. I need your help, baby girl. I'm stuck and I can't move on unless you help me."

"Anything, Dad. Just tell me what you need me to do," she said fervently.

"Get the killers, Simone. See that they spend the rest of their lives in jail. If you don't, I'll never be at peace. Do you hear me? I'll never be at peace." His voice became a roar and his face twisted with rage.

"Save me, Simone." Skeletal hands reached out toward her. She gasped and scooted back away from the headstone, but the hands kept coming and wrapped around her neck. Cold ghostly fingers squeezed tight, making it difficult for her to scream out her terror.

She awoke and jerked up with a deep gasp. Her breathing came in rapid pants and the horror of the dream still raced through her. Tears burned at her eyes as she thought of the beginning of the dream, when her father's pleas to her had been so heart-breaking. She didn't want to even think about the end of the dream. That man, that angry monster who had tried to strangle her, wasn't her loving father.

Still, the nightmare reminded her that she needed to do whatever she could to help find Leo Styler and she believed the answers to so many things were in Jared Garner.

And today she would get access to his interviews. At that thought a burst of adrenaline raced through her and she jumped out of bed.

An hour later she had showered and dressed in a pair of jeans and a coral-colored sleeveless blouse. She sat at the table with a cup of coffee and a toasted bagel in front of her, counting down the minutes to the meeting with Brad Howard.

As she ate, she thought about what her sister had said the day before about sensing some kind of attraction between her and Brad. Of course, the idea was utterly ridiculous.

He was just a very hot-looking FBI agent in town to do a job. All she really wanted from Agent Howard was answers that would lead to both of the teenagers in jail and eventually convicted for their crimes. It was the only way her father would find peace. It was the only way she would find some semblance of peace. And hopefully when that all happened, the nightmares would stop.

At nine thirty she left her condo. She carried

with her a legal pad so she could take notes and her purse. At precisely ten she walked into the police station and asked for Brad.

When he came out to greet her and lead her back to his office, she couldn't help but notice how his black pants fit his slim waist and long legs and how his gray dress shirt emphasized his broad shoulders.

He carried himself with the confidence of a man sure of himself. She'd always found a confident man attractive, but only if that self-assurance didn't border on arrogance. In Agent Howard's case, she didn't know enough about him to know if he was an arrogant man or not. In any case, she shouldn't care. He was simply the man in charge of a criminal case, a case where her father and uncle had been murdered.

When they reached the small space he worked from, there were two chairs on one side of the desk and the computer screen was turned toward the chairs.

Simone took the chair closer to the wall. Brad closed the office door and then sat next to her. Simone was instantly aware of his nearness, not as the FBI agent who might help her, but as a handsome man whose cologne tantalized her. It was a scent of something spicy and slightly mysterious.

"I have to confess I wrestled with myself all night long about having you here today," he said.

His eyes were a golden green today and he held her gaze steadily.

She leaned forward and placed the legal pad on the desk in front of her. "Why would you have any doubts? I'm hoping I'll be able to give you some insight that will further the investigation."

"Ultimately that's why I didn't call you to cancel this viewing," he replied. "However, I want you to understand that this access to these files is highly unusual and I need to have your promise that you won't take what you see or hear on them outside of this room."

"I can promise that," she replied. He held her gaze for several long moments, as if gauging if he could trust her or not. He must have been satisfied with what he saw in her for he turned to the computer.

"I figured I'd start with the first interview with Jared and his parents." He pushed several buttons on the computer and then an image of Jared, his parents and Brad in a large interview room came into view. Jared's lawyer sat in the background.

Simone leaned forward once again and grabbed her legal pad. She then withdrew a pen from her purse as she waited for the video to begin.

And then it was playing. Simone intently watched the interplay between all the people. She wrote down her impressions and thoughts as it played.

Simone had a good understanding of the human mind. She was also good at picking up cues and tells in behavior, behavior that often occurred in people in an effort to hide real emotions.

She knew that Jared's parents, Rob and Marilyn, owned a furniture store and that Jared had a grandmother who lived overseas. She also knew Jared's parents had been desperately making arrangements to send him overseas to escape the charges against him. Fortunately, he had been arrested before that could actually happen.

The interview lasted about an hour. "Thoughts?" Brad immediately asked when it was finished. "Opinions?"

She frowned. It had been a bit difficult to stay completely focused on the tape as she had found Brad's closeness to her a bit distracting. His body heat had radiated toward her and a couple of times his arm had brushed against hers, shocking her as pleasant tingles had rushed through her.

"I'd like to see more before I tell you what I'm thinking. Do you have additional video of Jared and his parents being interviewed?" she asked.

He nodded and pulled up a new file and opened a new video of the same five people. Once again, she did her best to focus on not only what was being said, but what was not said, which could be equally as revealing.

The video was a little over an hour and a half

long, and by the time they were finished, it was nearing one thirty. "You want to take a break and let me treat you to lunch?" he surprised her by asking. "There's a little deli around the corner that serves great sandwiches, and to be perfectly honest, I skipped dinner last night and so I'm starving."

"You don't have to take me to lunch," she protested.

"Really, Simone, I'd like to."

It was the first time he'd called her by her first name and she was surprised by how much she liked her name on his lips. "I only had a bagel for breakfast, so lunch sounds good."

"Then let's get out of here." They didn't speak again until they stepped outside of the building.

"Ah, fresh air," he said. "I love spring and early summer. What about you?" They fell into step side by side in a leisurely pace down the sidewalk.

"I prefer summer and winter," she replied.

"Ah, a woman of extremes," he said.

"Not really. There are just so many storms in the spring and fall, and I'm definitely a bit of a scaredy-cat when it comes to thunder and lightning."

A touch of emotion rose up in her chest. "I can't tell you how many times when I was little that my dad would hold me and rock me in a rocking chair I had next to my bed until the storm outside passed."

To her surprise, Brad reached out and touched the back of her hand. It was brief, but she knew his intent was to comfort. "I'm so sorry, Simone. I'm so damned sorry about what happened to your father and your uncle."

"Thanks. I'm just hoping we can get these two killers in prison where they belong. Just imagine how many more people they would have killed if they hadn't been found out. Just imagine if Leo is still out there killing people."

"Now, that's the stuff of my nightmares," he said ruefully.

Their talk stopped as he led the way into the little restaurant. It was a typical deli with a long counter and different kinds of meats and cheeses in a refrigerated display case. Small tables were scattered around the space and a huge handwritten menu blackboard offered a variety of sandwiches and a special of the day. Today the special was a cup of tomato basil soup and a turkey-avocado sandwich. Since it was late for lunch and too early for dinner, only a few of the tables were occupied.

"I'm sure this isn't exactly the kind of place you usually eat at," Brad said. "But over the last couple of months I've tried pretty much everything on the menu here and I can tell you it's all good."

She looked at him curiously. "What makes you think this kind of place is out of my wheelhouse? There are many days when I eat in the college cafeteria or I grab a sandwich at a deli near the campus."

"I just figured with your family background you

were accustomed to a finer dining experience," he replied.

She laughed. "It's obvious you don't know me at all. I'm really just a nerdy professor."

He smiled. "Then maybe I'll get to know you better over lunch."

For some reason his words caused a pleasant rivulet of warmth to rush through her. She quickly broke eye contact with him and instead looked up at the menu.

Minutes later they were seated at a table in the back with their lunch before them. Simone had ordered a turkey-and-cheese sandwich and Brad had ordered a ham and swiss. They both had chips and sodas.

"You want to talk about what you've seen so far on the videos?" he asked.

She frowned thoughtfully. "Not yet. You said you have more video of Jared being interviewed with his parents?"

"I have two more, but unfortunately I'm not going to be able to show them to you today. I have some meetings later this afternoon that I need to attend."

"Would I be able to view those tomorrow?" she asked.

"I can set you up to see them tomorrow at the same time as today. Does that work for you?"

"That definitely works for me," she agreed. This

close to him, she noticed that his eyelashes were sinfully long. He had an intense way of gazing at her, as if he were trying to delve into her very soul. If she was a criminal with something to hide, she would find his gaze quite daunting. "Thankfully I finished the last of my daytime classes and I'm not working through the summer," she added.

"Do you enjoy teaching psychology classes?" he asked.

"I love it, although for the last couple of years my schedule has become pretty heavy. Everyone likes to take classes in psychology and then three years ago I added courses in deviant behaviors and the criminal mind. What I didn't expect was for those classes to become so popular. I'm just grateful I only have a couple of night classes left to finish up and then I have two months free."

When she got nervous, she tended to talk too much and she flushed as she realized that was what she was doing. "I'm sorry. I'm doing all the talking here. So, what about you? Do you like what you do?"

"I feel like I was destined to hunt down killers." He looked at her for a moment and then stared at someplace just over her head. "When I was twelve, my mother was killed by a serial killer."

Simone gasped. "Oh my God, I'm so sorry."

He smiled at her. "Thank you, but it was a long

time ago. But it set me on the course of what I wanted to do with my life."

"Did the authorities catch the person who killed your mother?" The fact that at one time in his life he'd probably felt the same emotions, the same pain that she felt somehow made her feel a strange connection with him.

"No, they didn't. He raped and killed six women in six days and then stopped the killing spree. He left few clues behind and the authorities were unable to arrest anyone for the crimes. It has remained a cold case. I'm just glad we were able to give you some answers about who killed your father, although it was no thanks to the profile I worked on."

"What do you mean?" She picked up a chip and popped it into her mouth.

"I spent so much time trying to tie your father and your uncle to the other two victims. I was convinced there had to be some connection between them and I spun my wheels trying to find it."

She smiled at him. "Don't beat yourself up. I did the same thing. I worked for hours trying to profile the killer but never guessed that it was two teenagers killing random victims."

She didn't want to talk murder anymore. She'd been immersed in it for the past six months. Now she found herself interested in the man seated across from her.

"So, tell me more about you. I know you live in

Washington, DC. Do you have a family there? A wife and children?"

"No, it's just me."

"So, you aren't married?" She wasn't sure how old he was, but he appeared to be in his midthirties or so.

"No. Got close once, but it fell apart before we could get to the altar. She thought I was already married to my job and she refused to marry a man she didn't believe would make her a priority. What about you? Have you ever been married?" Once again, his eyes held an intensity that threatened to half steal her breath away.

"No. My last relationship broke up a little over a year ago and I haven't really dated anyone since then." She smiled at him. "I, too, have been accused of being married to my job."

For the next few minutes, they ate and small talked about the weather and life in Chicago. She told him about the sudden appearance of two mystery heirs attempting to claim part of the family business and he asked questions about Colton Connections.

She was surprised by how easy he was to talk to. He'd always appeared stiff and professional when he'd met with the family about the murder. But today he was a bit softer and far more approachable than she would have thought. She could have sat and talked to him forever, but she was also aware that he needed to get back to his very important work.

When the meal was finished, they stepped outside into the bright sunshine. "Thank you, Agent Howard, for allowing me the opportunity to view the tapes, and thank you so much for lunch," she replied.

"No problem, and please call me Brad."

Once again, he'd surprised her. "How about I call you Brad only when the two of us are alone?"

He smiled at her, a wide smile that slightly crinkled the outward corners of his eyes and filled his features with a heart-stopping warmth. "That works. And I'll see you again tomorrow morning at ten."

"You can count on it," she said with a smile of her own.

A few minutes later Simone was heading home with thoughts of the attractive FBI man in her mind. She should be thinking about the taped evidence she'd seen, but thoughts of Brad intruded.

Today she'd seen pieces of the man and not the agent in charge of her father's murder. And she'd liked what she'd seen. She tried to tell herself she was eager to go into the station the next day to see more video, and she was. But the truth of the matter was she was also eager to spend more time with Brad.

She needed to get her head in a better space and

focus on the fact that it didn't matter how attracted she was to him. Ultimately he was doing a job, and when the job was finished, he'd go back to his life in Washington, DC. Besides, what would a very hot FBI agent find attractive about a nerdy professor who was scared of storms?

Brad left the deli and Simone, and then headed back to headquarters. He shouldn't have had lunch with her, and he definitely shouldn't have gone into any details about his personal life. The fact that he'd been reluctant for the lunch to end was definitely problematic.

In all his years of working as a homicide detective, he'd always managed to keep professional and personal very separate. There was just something about Simone Colton...

Maybe it was because her bright blue eyes emanated not only strength and intelligence, but also a soft vulnerability that somehow drew him in. Or perhaps it was because her hair looked so shiny and soft and touchable and her lips had a small pout that looked extremely kissable.

Jeez, what was wrong with him? It was definitely time he wound up this case and got back to his life in DC—his very lonely life in DC.

He shoved this thought away. He knew part of the flaw he suffered from was most of the time he preferred to spend time in the minds of killers rather than in the minds of ordinary people.

At thirty-six years old he'd pretty much written off love and marriage for himself. It had also become more difficult to have a group of buddies to hang out with.

Most of his friends were now married with families of their own and Brad no longer felt comfortable being a third wheel in their lives. The exception to that was his partner, Russ, and his wife, Janie, who always invited him to dinner or to spend special occasions with them.

The single men who worked with him tended to be bitter, burned-out cops who drank too much and talked about their ex-wives and taking early retirement.

He had no idea what he found so appealing about Simone, but it was an attraction he certainly didn't intend to explore. In fact, as he settled back down in his office, he consciously shoved all thoughts of her out of his mind.

As soon as he settled back in, he made a series of phone calls to check with the men who were out on the streets looking for Leo Styler. The kid had to be somewhere, but so far they hadn't been able to find his location.

He pulled up a photo from a social media profile. Styler looked like a punk wannabe. He was fond of camo pants and black T-shirts. A heavy gold chain and lock that could be used as a weapon hung around his neck, but Brad sensed they were used just to intimidate others.

In talking to some of Leo's peers, Brad had gotten a picture of a kid who wanted to connect with members of the opposite sex, but his antisocial behavior was a big turnoff.

Neither of the boys were big in academics, which was why they were attending a community college rather than the kind of colleges their parents could afford. However, the two boys were into the sport of mag-fed paintball gaming.

Brad had needed to educate himself in the sport when he heard about it. He'd learned that *mag-fed* meant magazine-fed paint guns, giving the player the experience of loading and shooting guns that were similar to the real thing. There were two such clubs in Chicago and Brad had men undercover and hanging around them in the hopes that Leo might show up at one of them. But so far the kid had been a no-show.

Brad didn't believe that Leo's parents had managed to get Leo out of the states and now his name was flagged, so it would be difficult for him to even get a bus ticket out of town. James and Miranda Styler professed they didn't know where their son was, but Brad was betting they were somehow keeping him funded so he had a motel or someplace to crash in and food to eat.

He had men sitting on the Styler home to see if the kid tried to sneak back home. Brad felt as if he had covered all the bases and it was just a matter of time before they got Leo behind bars.

The day was long with the task force meeting to update each other. Brad was the liaison between the two FBI agents who had come with him from DC and the three Chicago detectives who had been lent to him during the investigation.

Unfortunately, there was no news. He had another interview scheduled with Jared and his parents the next day. He was hoping to get a confession out of Jared so that when they found Leo they could book him on murder charges.

It was almost dark when he left the police station and headed back to the hotel that he'd called home for the past two months. He stopped in the deli and grabbed a sandwich to take with him and then walked on.

Minutes later he was in his hotel room. The room was nothing fancy, but it had a good king-size bed, a small round table with chairs, a television with cable and a mini fridge.

He made himself a cup of coffee in the one-cup coffee maker and then sank down at the table and opened the sack containing his sandwich.

As he ate, all the events of the murders rushed through his head. For months the officials had worked the case believing that the killer was perhaps a family member, a disgruntled worker at the family business or a business enemy.

With Colton Connections having fifty full-time employees, it had been a time-consuming process for the Chicago PD to interview each and every one of them.

Then Larry Kidwell and Jonathon Paxton had been shot, using the same MO as in the Colton case. The two businessmen had been killed in the parking lot outside their business warehouse, just like the Colton men. At that point the FBI had been called in. Nobody had anticipated that the killers were a couple of kids.

Brad had just finished with his sandwich when a knock fell on his door. Even though he suspected who it was, he still grabbed his gun before opening the door.

FBI agent Russ Dodd grinned at him and held up a six-pack of beer. "Feel like a cold brew before bedtime?"

"Sounds good to me." He ushered Russ in and to the table. Russ was also from DC and had worked with Brad for the last six years. The two men had both a good professional relationship and a strong friendship. Russ now slid one of the cold brews across the table to Brad. They both opened their beers and then settled back in their chairs.

Russ took a deep drink and then released a deep

sigh. "Well, another night ends without that little punk Leo in jail," he said.

"Yeah, and no confession from Jared."

Russ snorted. "You'll never get a confession from him as long as his parents are hovering around, answering questions for him and telling him to keep his mouth shut."

"Don't remind me," Brad replied. "How's your family doing?"

Russ grinned, causing the freckles on his face to dance with the gesture. "They're doing okay. They miss me, but I FaceTime once a day with the two kids and then I FaceTime Janie right before I go to bed."

"You're a damned lucky man that you found a woman who supports your work," Brad replied.

"Trust me, I know how lucky I am." He released a small laugh. "And if I threaten to forget it, Janie reminds me just how lucky I am." Russ took another drink, and when he finished, he eyed Brad curiously. "Speaking of women, I couldn't help but notice you had Simone Colton in your office for a long time today. What's up with that?"

"You know she's a psychologist and she's studied extensively in the area of deviant human behavior."

"And?" Russ raised one of his light red eyebrows.

"And I'm allowing her to view the taped interviews we've conducted with Jared so far. What I'm hoping is that she'll pick up on something that I've missed, something that might help me crack Jared."

"Interesting," Russ replied with a grin. "And it doesn't hurt that she's very attractive."

Brad felt himself flush with a sudden heat that fired through him. "That has absolutely nothing to do with my decision to allow her to watch the interviews. I'm just looking for a way to break this case. If we could get Jared to talk, then he might be able to lead us to where Leo is hiding out."

"Right now, his parents are alibiing Jared for the night of the murder," Russ replied. "There's no way you're going to get through them to get Jared to confess to anything. Hell, he's now saying that he won't even talk to you at all without them in the interrogation room. You're never going to break that kid."

"Thanks for the vote of confidence," Brad replied drily.

"Hey, I hope Simone Colton can see something we've missed. Jared and Leo definitely need to be taken off the streets for a very long time. Even though they're both young, they are also cold-blooded murderers."

For the next few minutes, the two kicked around theories of where Leo might be hiding out. When their beer cans were empty, Russ stood. "I'll get out of here so you can get some sleep. Besides, I need to call Janie before it gets too late."

Russ grabbed the four remaining beers and then Brad walked him to the door. "I'll see you tomorrow, Russ."

"Yeah, and maybe it will be a good day and we'll get Styler under arrest."

"That would definitely be a stellar day," Brad replied.

An hour later Brad had showered and gotten into bed. The lights from outside the hotel room drifted in through a crack in his curtains and he stared up at the ceiling where shadows formed an intricate pattern.

His mind suddenly formed a picture of Simone. Surely his interest in her was only because he hoped she might be able to move the investigation forward and nothing more.

He'd been far too open with her today. It was just that she'd been so easy to talk to. He'd definitely felt a spark with her, a spark he hadn't felt for a very long time and one he needed to douse as soon as possible.

Tomorrow he'd make sure he was more professional when he was with her. He wouldn't invite conversation unless it had something to do with the case. He needed to keep clear boundaries where she was concerned.

As beautiful as he found Simone, as drawn to her as he found himself, ultimately he was here to catch a killer and nothing more.

Chapter 3

Simone walked briskly toward the police station, eager to have another opportunity to view more video of Jared Garner and his parents as Jared was being interrogated. She'd come to several conclusions about what she believed the dynamics were between the three, dynamics that had formed Jared's character. However, before she shared her conclusions with Brad, she wanted to see the rest of the videos he had to confirm her findings.

When she arrived, Brad greeted her and led her back to his office. Today he again wore a pair of black pants, but this time a dark green button-down shirt stretched across his broad shoulders. He also wore his shoulder holster with his gun.

When she'd dressed that morning, she'd pulled on a summer dress in shades of pink, a dress that had earned her many compliments whenever she'd worn it. She'd also applied a little more mascara than usual. It was only when she was putting on a pink shiny lip gloss that she wondered what in the heck she was doing.

She was dressed more for a date than for a professional consultation. She was conscious of Brad's gaze sweeping the length of her as she sat in the same chair as she had the day before. His gaze felt like a caress and warmed her in a delicious and slightly disturbing kind of way. Definitely not the way to keep things professional between them.

"Shall we get started?" he asked as he cued up a video.

"Ready when you are," she replied. She tried not to notice the attractive scent of Brad as she focused on the computer screen, where the video had begun.

In the first interview she had seen of Jared, he'd been dressed in a pair of khaki slacks and a kelly green designer shirt. He'd had a wholesome appeal with his blond hair styled in a short preppy style and his smile full of straight white teeth.

In this video he was clad in an ill-fitting jailhouse-orange jumpsuit. His hair had grown out a bit, but the one thing that remained the same was the soulless look in his blue eyes. They were eyes that said the person behind them was badly broken.

There was no question that even though she tried to focus solely on the interview, she found Brad a distraction. She didn't understand why she seemed to be so hyperaware of him.

There was a decided difference about him today. Where he had shown some warmth and friendliness the day before, he was strictly professional today. He didn't invite any idle conversation and that was fine with her. That was the way it should be.

They watched two more taped videos and then Brad looked at her curiously. "That's all I have to show you. Now I'm very interested in what you can tell me about what you've seen."

She flipped to the beginning of the notes she'd taken on her legal pad and scanned the things she'd written down both that day and the day before.

"You do realize these are just my own impressions?" she began.

"Yes, but I consider them expert impressions," he replied, and a hint of warmth filled his gaze.

She smiled. "Let's see if you feel the same way after you hear them." She cleared her throat and once again looked at her notes. "It's obvious to me that Jared holds a tremendous amount of anger directed toward his parents. He appears calm in their presence, but his anger bubbles just beneath the surface."

She had written down the time stamps on each video where she had seen the tells of Jared's underlying rage. "I suspect either one or both of his parents are physically and mentally abusive to him." She shared the times she had seen the indications and body language to support that and Brad wrote down the times on his own legal pad.

He then leaned back in his chair and looked at her with obvious curiosity. "Tell me more."

She didn't know if he was simply indulging her or if he was really taking in her thoughts and theories and actually considering them. He was difficult to read. "I also don't believe Jared is the mastermind of these murders. I think probably Leo offered Jared the friendship and compassion that was lacking in Jared's life. Jared strikes me as a follower, and I think if approached correctly, he could be reasoned with."

"It's difficult to get much of anything out of him with him insisting that his parents be there in the interrogation room. His father is very overbearing and his mother is just as bad. Jared seems afraid to answer any questions without their approval," Brad replied.

"You need to try to appeal to Jared not just with questions about the crimes, but also show an interest in his life…his likes and dislikes. Show him friendship and compassion. I believe that's what might break him despite his parents' influence."

Brad tapped the end of his pen on his notepad, checked his watch and then gazed at her thoughtfully. "Simone, I need to wrap this up for now, but I'd like to take you to dinner this evening and discuss all this further."

"Oh…" She looked at him in complete surprise. Of all the things he might have said to her, an invitation to dinner was the very last thing she'd expected from him.

"I'd definitely like to pick your brain a little bit more about things," he added. "So, would you let me take you to dinner this evening?"

Of course, he wasn't asking her out for a real date. It was more of a professional consultation over a meal. "How about we meet at my sister's restaurant, True?"

"That sounds good to me. A couple of the Chicago PD officers took me there to eat when I first got to town and the food was fantastic. Shall we say around six?"

"Six sounds perfect," she agreed. She didn't even try to analyze why her heart fluttered just a little bit at the thoughts of the night to come.

"Great, then I look forward to it." He stood and she did as well. He walked her out and then they said their goodbyes. He disappeared back into the police station and she headed back home.

He had given her no clues to indicate that dinner would be anything but a professional collaboration, but that didn't stop her from feeling just a little bit giddy at thoughts of sharing dinner with him.

What was wrong with her? Why was Brad Howard affecting her in a way she hadn't felt for a very long time? Surely it was only because he was treating her like an intelligent woman whose opinions mattered.

That was what had been lacking in her relationship with Wayne Jamison. Wayne had often dismissed her thoughts and opinions. It had been vitally important to him that he be the smarter, the funnier and the more respected of the couple.

Eventually she had just grown tired of being dismissed by him. She was a strong, independent and smart woman and she deserved a man who respected her on all those levels. However, at this time in her life, she wasn't even sure a man like that existed.

At quarter till five she showered and got ready for her date. No, not a date, she corrected herself firmly. It was nothing more than two professionals sharing a business dinner.

So, why then did nerves twist her stomach so tight? Why did she feel so excited about the night to come? She pulled on a pair of black slacks and a forest green blouse that somehow made her think of Brad's eyes.

There was no question she felt a physical attraction toward Brad. What living, breathing woman wouldn't? It was just a reminder that she'd been alone for too long. There were several men at the college who had invited her out over the past year, but she'd declined all of them. Maybe it was time she began dating again.

She missed being in a relationship. She was tired of eating alone each night. She wanted somebody to share special moments with, to do something as simple as share a beautiful sunset or talk about the ordinary events that made up a day. She wanted a snuggle bunny at night, somebody who could take her breath away with a single kiss.

Maybe that was why she felt a bit vulnerable to Brad Howard. She was just lonely and he was giving her a little bit of attention. He seemed to be actually interested in hearing her opinions and it felt good.

Even though it wasn't a date, she took extra care with her makeup and made sure she looked nice. She needed to take special care if they were meeting at True. She certainly wanted Tatum to be proud of her whenever she visited the restaurant.

She arrived at there at exactly six o'clock. She stepped inside and immediately saw Brad seated at the bar. For several moments he didn't see her and she took the opportunity to watch him.

He looked bigger...stronger than the other men at the bar. It wasn't in his physique, but it was the way he wore his confidence. He appeared to command the space around him more than any of the other men seated there.

While she found that appealing in theory, she wondered if that confidence could be arrogant. If it could be demeaning and hurtful.

At that moment he turned and saw her. A wide smile curved his lips and her heart fluttered way more than it should. He stood from the stool, threw a few dollars on the bar and then hurried over to her.

"Have you been waiting long?" she asked.

"No, not at all," he assured her. "Our table is ready if you are."

"I'm ready," she replied.

He took her by the elbow and led her through the main dining room. As they walked, she looked around for her sister but didn't see her anywhere.

Their table was a two-top in a corner in the back of the restaurant. It was semi-secluded, the perfect place for a romantic interlude, or in this case, the perfect place to talk about all things murder.

The minute they settled in, a waitress arrived to take their drink orders. She ordered a glass of white wine and he ordered a scotch and soda. Once the drinks had been delivered and dinner orders had been taken, he offered her that smile that warmed her from head to toe. "So, how was the rest of your afternoon today?"

"It was fine. I have a lecture tomorrow evening at the college, so I spent some time going over my notes," she replied. "What about you?"

"We had a little bit of excitement. An anonymous phone call came in telling us Leo had been spotted at a McDonald's restaurant. Several squad cars descended on the place, but there was no Leo. The officers showed his picture around and none of the staff or customers had seen him."

"Do you get a lot of false alarms like that?" she asked, disappointed that yet another day was drawing to an end without one of her father's murderers in custody.

"Unfortunately, we do. Anytime we have a case where we've set up a TIPS line and have shown the suspect's picture all over the news and on social media, we get a lot of calls. We check out each and every single one, but unfortunately, they are mostly crank calls."

"It just seems like it's been forever since the murders occurred and there's still no justice for my uncle and my father. I still can't believe they're really gone. I always dreamed of my father walking me down the aisle on my wedding day and being a terrific and loving grandpa to my children."

To her horror, tears suddenly burned in her eyes and her ever-present grief closed up the back of her throat. She quickly looked down at the tablecloth in an effort to gain back her control.

To her stunned surprise, Brad reached out and grabbed one of her hands in his. She looked up at him and instantly wanted to fall into the soft pools of compassion his eyes offered her.

"We're going to get him, Simone." He gave her hand a gentle squeeze. "I swear we're going to get him, and both Leo and Jared are going to spend the rest of their lives in prison for the murder of your father and uncle." He gave her hand another squeeze and then released it.

She quickly managed to get her emotions back under control and took a sip of her wine. "Sorry, I didn't mean to get all emotional on you."

"Please, don't apologize. Even getting the two of them in jail won't take your grief away, Simone. I wish there was something magical I could do that would accomplish that. I'd love to see your beautiful eyes without the grief that shines so sadly from them. Unfortunately, it's my experience that only time will help."

He'd called her eyes beautiful and had made her heart flutter once again. She tried to ignore that and looked at him curiously. "Do you still grieve for your mother?"

"To me, grief has been a funny kind of animal. When the crime first happened, my grief for my mother was like a hard rock concert. It was all bass and cymbals crashing in my head. Now it's more like a nighttime lullaby that isn't sung every night, but occasionally it whispers through my head on a wave of soft notes."

"That's nice," she said. "But I'm still in the rock concert stage."

"I know, and I hate that for you."

She took a sip of her wine and then set the wine-glass back down. "I just feel like I can't even start the healing process until the murderers are put away where they can never hurt anyone again."

She would do anything she could to help Brad get the two teenagers in jail. She needed to think about what exactly she could do to hurry this case along. She definitely would do anything to stop the horrifying nightmares that tortured her at night.

By the time dinner arrived, all talk of grief was gone. Instead, the conversation revolved around more pleasant topics. They talked about favorite sports—he was a baseball fan and she loved foot-ball. They spoke about favorite music and what they enjoyed watching on television—she liked jazz and he liked old rock and roll, and they both enjoyed watching crime dramas.

Someplace in the back of Brad's mind, he knew they should discuss the case and her insights more, but right now he was just enjoying watching her relax.

She looked beautiful in her slacks and the forest green blouse, a color that only seemed to emphasize the bright blue of her eyes. He was grateful that as their conversation had continued her eyes had lost some of their sadness.

"This is the best steak I've ever eaten," he said as they continued with the meal.

"They get great reviews on their steaks, but I've never eaten one."

"You're not into steak?" he asked curiously.

"It's okay. I just like chicken better," she replied.

"I'm assuming your sister is an amazing cook. Do you enjoy cooking as well?"

"Absolutely not," she replied and then laughed.

It was the first time he'd heard her laughter and he loved the low, slightly throaty sound of it. "That was pretty definite," he said with a laugh of his own.

"Tatum always enjoyed puttering in the kitchen. I've never particularly enjoyed being there. Normally my schedule stays fairly busy, so it's easy for me to grab lunch out and order in for dinner," she explained.

"Why psychology?" he asked.

She set her fork down and took a drink of her wine. "When I was in high school, I was stalked by a boy. His name was Bill Jacobs. I was in my junior year and he had already graduated. I dated him for a month and then broke up with him because he was too controlling. After that, whenever I went out with somebody else, Bill was always there. Even when I went out with my girlfriends, we'd spy his car following several car lengths behind us. It was creepy and it went on for a couple of months."

"Did he ever get violent with you?" Brad asked. The idea of anyone ever hurting her certainly didn't sit well with him.

She took another drink of her wine and then shook her head. "No, it never escalated into anything like that, although I was afraid it might. Eventually it just stopped and I never saw him again, but I was always intrigued by what drove him. Then when I got to college, I took a course in psychology and realized that was my true passion…to try to understand the human mind."

"It always amazes me how events in our childhoods form the people we become," he replied.

"And that's definitely what drew me to psychology," she replied.

"Did you ever think about going into private practice?"

"I considered it, but I really enjoy teaching. It's very rewarding to think I'm educating young minds and maybe some of my students will go on to become good therapists or whatever."

He smiled at her. "I have the utmost respect for teachers."

"And I have the utmost respect for law enforcement," she replied.

For a long moment their gazes remained locked and Brad felt a surge of emotions fill him. It wasn't just physical attraction. It was more than that. It was a desire to get to know her better, a need to protect her and do everything in his power to make her happy.

It scared the hell out of him. It had been a very long time since he'd felt this kind of interest in a woman. And she was definitely the wrong woman for him to feel this way about.

She broke the eye contact and he cleared his throat. "So, what dessert do you recommend?" he asked.

"It depends on what you like. My favorite is the raspberry torte, but honestly you can't go wrong with any of the desserts here," she said.

When the waitress arrived to clear their dinner dishes, he ordered two of the tortes and two cups of coffee. Once their desserts arrived, he felt the need to distance himself by taking the conversation back to the interview videos he'd played for her.

"Have you had any more thoughts about Jared?" he asked.

"I spent part of the afternoon going over my notes, and I stand by what I told you," she replied.

He hated that her eyes darkened. "So, maybe it's time I take a different approach in the interview room. Be more friendly with the kid and try to build a relationship with him despite his parents' presence. I've been playing bad cop and what you're suggesting is that I need to play good cop."

She smiled. "Maybe honey is better than vinegar in this particular case. I have a feeling he's been fairly lonely for most of his life. He had to have been to hook up with a friend like Leo." She placed her napkin on top of the table. "Could you please excuse me for a minute?"

"Of course." He stood as she did and watched as she wove her way through the tables to disappear into a side alcove where the restrooms were located.

He frowned thoughtfully and picked up his coffee cup. Maybe she was right. He was definitely not getting anywhere with Jared playing the tough cop. Still, he had to admit it hurt his ego just a little bit to realize it took an outsider to see things he and his team might have missed.

He'd been the one conducting all the interviews with Jared and his parents, and there was no question that so far he'd felt as if he were spinning his wheels.

Funny, it was much easier to think about a serial killer than to examine all the inappropriate emotions that Simone stirred inside him.

Maybe the real problem was that he was just a lonely man and he would have reacted positively to any attractive woman he spent a little bit of time with. Once he finally got back home, maybe he needed to make more of an effort to have a little social time, to maybe pursue a dating life once again.

He was about to take another drink of coffee when a commotion near the restrooms drew his attention. He was surprised to see Rob and Marilyn

Garner, who had apparently just been seated at a table, and Simone.

Simone looked like a deer in the headlights as Rob rose from his chair and pointed his finger in her face. "My son is innocent and you need to mind your business, you Colton bitch," he yelled.

Brad jumped out of his chair and hurried toward them. He didn't hear what Simone said in return, but Rob took a step closer to her and his finger became a fist.

"You've just stirred up a lot of trouble for yourself, missy," Rob raged. "You'd better watch your back, you hear me?"

Simone stumbled backward. Brad grabbed her by the arm and pulled her away. "You need to sit down right now, Mr. Garner," he yelled at the obviously angry man, and then he quickly led Simone back to their table.

She was visibly upset. Her face was ashen and her entire body trembled. "I…I came out of the restroom and saw them. I just asked them if they would sit down with me sometime and let me ask them a few questions. He…he just exploded."

Dammit, how had this happened and why in hell had she approached them in the first place? "Simone, you shouldn't have talked to them."

"I… I just wanted to…" Her voice trailed off.

"Simone, you need to stay away from those people. Rob Garner is a loose cannon and there's no telling what he might do if he sees you as a potential threat to his son," Brad said.

Her cheeks finally began to refill with a touch of color. "I'm so embarrassed. I was just so…so shocked by his reaction." She reached up and tucked a strand of hair behind her ear and he couldn't help but notice that her hand still trembled.

"I almost feel sorry for Jared growing up with that man," she finally said.

"Still, you shouldn't have talked to them."

Before he could say anything else, Tatum Colton appeared beside their table. She placed a hand on Simone's shoulder. "Simone, are you okay?" she asked worriedly.

"I'm fine," Simone replied, although her voice still held a slight tremor.

Tatum frowned. "Some of the staff told me what just happened. I'm going to get security to ask the Garners to leave."

"Oh, please don't do that, Tatum. It will just make another scene, and besides, Brad and I are finished, so we'll be leaving," Simone replied.

"I didn't even realize you were here. Why didn't you tell me you were going to be here this evening?" Tatum asked. Her gaze shot to Brad and then back to Simone.

"We were just having a…uh…consultation together." Simone's cheeks dusted with a blush. "But we're ready to leave now. Right, Brad?"

"Definitely," he agreed. They had pretty much finished up with their dessert and coffee, and there was really no reason to linger any longer. Even if Simone had wanted to linger for another cup of coffee, which he was sure she didn't, he would have wanted to get her out of here as soon as possible anyway.

He wanted to get her as far away as possible from Rob Garner. He wanted to yell at her for speaking to them at all, for insinuating herself into a place where she didn't belong. But she looked so shocked, so utterly vulnerable at the moment, the last thing he wanted to do was come down too hard on her.

He paid their tab and then together they left the restaurant. They stepped out into the evening air and simply stood on the sidewalk away from the crowd waiting to get into the restaurant.

She still appeared traumatized. Once again, she tucked a strand of her hair behind her ear and he noticed that her hand still trembled. "Are you sure you're okay?" he finally asked. He put his arm around her shoulders and pulled her closer to his side.

She stayed there for a long moment and then stepped away from him. She nodded. "I'm all right, just still a little bit shaken up and shocked."

"Simone, you can't try to talk to them again. It should be apparent to you now that Rob Garner is not the kind of man to mess with," he replied. "I don't want you to go anywhere near him again."

"I was very civil when I approached them. All I asked was if they'd be willing to sit down with me and have a short chat."

"I'm sure you were civil, but Rob Garner is not," he replied. "And I know you want to help, but you need to step back now and leave it all up to us."

She released a deep sigh. "Oh, well, aside from that, it was a lovely evening and I really enjoyed having dinner with you."

"I enjoyed it, too," he replied. "Can I take you home?"

"No, I'm fine to get home on my own," she replied and offered him a beautiful smile. "Thank you again, Brad, and I hope you'll keep me updated on the case."

"Of course I will." He already wanted to see her again. Not as professionals meeting to discuss Jared Garner, but rather as a man and a woman getting to know each other better.

And that was why he shouldn't see her again. The timing and circumstances were all wrong for him to be distracted in a romance that ultimately would go nowhere.

They said their goodbyes, and as he watched her walk away from him, he thought about how Rob Garner had yelled at her, basically threatening her life.

It made Brad worry for her. He hoped she stayed as far away from Rob as possible. He wanted Rob to forget all about Simone. But the truth of the matter was he had no idea what Garner might do now that Simone was on his radar. And that scared the hell out of him.

Chapter 4

"I'm not sure my client is going to agree to this." Roger Albright, Jared Garner's lawyer, frowned at Brad. The two were seated in an interview room.

Albright was a tall, dark-haired man who looked like big money in a three-piece suit that Brad knew cost more than Brad's monthly salary. The man even smelled expensive. However, Brad found him incredibly arrogant and condescending.

"Legally his parents don't have to be in the room when I question your client. At nineteen years old, Jared is an adult," Brad reminded the man. "I've been quite accommodating to your client by allowing them to sit in."

"I'm aware of that," Albright said with cool disdain. "However, my client has told you he doesn't intend to speak to you without them present in the room."

"As you know, we have another interview scheduled with Jared in an hour and I'm not going to allow his parents in the room. I'm not accommodating that request anymore going forward."

Albright raised one of his dark brows. "You do realize it's possible Jared won't cooperate without them there."

"He hasn't cooperated with them in the room. I certainly hope you encourage your client to start to fully cooperate with us. At the very least he's on the hook for kidnapping charges and he's also going to be charged with four murders," Brad said.

Albright waved his hand dismissively. "All false charges. Jared has a solid alibi for the nights of the murders."

Brad nearly snorted in derision. Jared's "alibi" was that he had been at a family function on the night the Colton men had been murdered, an alibi provided strictly by Rob and a handful of other family members, and one that was on very shaky grounds.

"I just wanted to inform you that today his parents are not welcome when I speak to Jared," Brad said.

"I'll let him know." Albright rose from his chair. "And I'll see you in an hour."

Brad remained seated at the table where he would soon be interrogating Jared. With Simone's observations fresh in his mind, he hoped to break through to Jared in a way he hadn't before.

It had been three days since he'd seen Simone, three days since they'd had dinner and she had been threatened by Rob Garner. Brad had called her yesterday just to check in with her. The conversation had been brief, but he had been glad just to hear her voice and to know she was doing okay.

He had a niggling worry about her. He had no idea if he should take the threats Rob had made to her in the restaurant seriously or not.

When he'd spoken to her on the phone, he'd reminded her to stay as far away from the Garners as possible, but he wasn't sure if she was taking his advice to heart or not. She was so desperate to get Jared and Leo sent to prison that he feared she wouldn't take her personal safety seriously.

However, he couldn't entertain thoughts of Simone right now. He needed to study the notes he'd written for this particular interrogation with Jared. He hoped like hell the kid would cooperate without his parents present.

There had been no more sightings of Leo. Brad had no idea how Leo was managing to exist off the grid. They had officers sitting on his parents' home and they'd interviewed the few friends the kid had. Nobody had seen him or appeared to be helping him in any way.

Somehow, someway, either his parents or Jared's parents had to be funneling Leo money, but the police had yet to figure out how. The kid was considered armed and dangerous, and his photo was still being flashed on the news and on all the social media platforms.

Forty minutes later Albright returned to the interview room. He greeted Brad once again and then sat in a chair just behind the one Jared would sit in.

Five minutes later Jared was led into the room by an officer. Clad in a jailhouse-orange jumpsuit and with shackles on his ankles and wrists, he looked especially young and vulnerable. But four men were dead due to this kid and his friend. That was the bottom line.

Once Jared was seated at the table, the officer unlocked Jared's wrist shackles and then stepped out of the room.

"Hi, Jared," Brad said.

"Why can't my parents be here? You've pretty much always let them be in here before." Jared's gaze skittered around the room nervously.

"We've been very good about granting your wish that they can occasionally be here when we talk to you, but today I just want to talk to you without them here," Brad explained.

Jared finally met his gaze. "I've already talked

to you, like, a hundred times. I got nothing else to say."

"I just wanted to get to know you a little better, Jared," Brad replied. "I've spoken to you a number of times, but I don't feel like I've gotten to know the real Jared. For the most part, you seem like a good kid. How are you finding life in jail?"

"The food sucks," Jared said. "And the bed sucks," he continued. "It's totally boring. The time goes really slow. They won't let me have my cell phone in here or anything."

"What do you like to do on your cell? Are you into any kinds of games on your phone?" Brad asked.

"I like Zombie Island and House of Thunder."

Brad frowned. "I'm not familiar with those. Tell me what they're about."

As Jared explained each of the games, Brad could tell he was starting to relax a bit. Brad was vaguely surprised to learn that in each of the games Jared identified with the "good" guys and tried to rid the environment of the bad people. So, what had happened that in real life he'd decided to be a bad guy? A murderer?

"I know you also enjoyed playing mag-fed paintball," Brad said when Jared had finished explaining the cell phone games he liked to play.

"Yeah, Leo got me into that. It's cool and we played whenever we got the chance." Jared frowned.

"My dad thought it was a stupid waste of time and money."

"I've noticed in our interviews that your father is pretty hard on you."

Jared's nostrils thinned and his eyes narrowed. "Yeah, so what?"

"I think maybe he's hard on you sometimes when you don't deserve it."

"My dad can be a real son of a bitch." The words exploded out of him as if forced out by a tremendous pressure. He then clamped his mouth shut as if sorry he had said that much. He looked at the wall just over Brad's head.

"It's okay, Jared. I get it. My dad was a real son of a bitch, too. Nothing I ever did pleased him. No matter how hard I tried, I couldn't do anything to make him happy with me. I felt like he didn't want me and he definitely didn't love me."

Jared stared at Brad for several long moments. "For real?"

"For real," Brad replied and held Jared's gaze. However, nothing could be further from the truth. Brad's father had been a loving, supportive man until he had passed away five years ago. But Brad would gladly lie in this moment if it was a lie that moved them closer to the truth in the case.

"Did your dad ever hit you?" Jared asked.

"He punched me a few times when he thought I needed it. It was nothing for him to smack me upside the head or slam my back with his fist. Does your dad hit you?"

Jared's eyes turned an icy blue. "Yeah."

Albright cleared his throat as if to warn Jared. Jared turned around and glared at the man. "I can say what I want here. You're my lawyer, not my father's," he said angrily.

Jared then turned back to Brad. "Yeah, my old man hits me. He punches me whenever he feels like it and my mother calls me a loser and a poor excuse for a son. She tells me she should have aborted me."

Brad was shocked by what the kid was sharing about his parents, but he didn't show it. "So, your friends must be really important to you as an escape from your home life," Brad said.

"I'm not stupid. I know you want me to talk about Leo."

Brad leaned forward. "I'm trying to understand your relationship with Leo. He's not like you, Jared. I sense that you have a good heart and I'm not sure if Leo does."

Jared shrugged. "He's been a good friend to me. He listens to me when I talk about my parents. He gets it and he gets me like nobody else ever has. He's my best friend."

"That's good that you found a friend like that. Where were the two of you planning on going?"

"What do you mean?"

Albright leaned forward. "Agent Howard, you're traveling in dangerous territory."

Brad looked at Jared innocently. "I don't know what's dangerous about what I just asked. We all know you and Leo had bug-out bags ready to go when you were arrested, so we know the two of you were planning on taking off somewhere."

When the FBI had burst into Leo's parents' basement, where the two boys had their "hangout," space, two bags were found. The bags had extra clothes, some cash and other items that the two boys might have needed for a life on the run.

"We were just planning on leaving home. We were ready to get away, but we never really talked about where we were going. If you want me to tell you where Leo is right now, I can't. You can beat me and everything, and I wouldn't be able to tell you. I don't know where he is or what he's doing." Jared frowned thoughtfully. "Sometimes he was kinda secretive, even with me."

"You know, it's possible I could get the authorities to allow you a little access to your phone for playing your games if you could think of anything that might help us find Leo," Brad said.

"Agent Howard, don't try to make deals with my client," Albright said.

"I just want to do something to help you, Jared," Brad continued, pointedly ignoring Albright. "Eventually Leo will be caught and I truly believe he's going to try to pin everything on you, Jared. He's going to throw you under the bus and I'd hate to see that happen to you. You've had enough people in your life who have let you down. I want to do right by you, Jared. I like you and I think you deserve a break. I just want you to think about things, and no matter if it's day or night, if you think of something that might help us and help yourself, let me know."

Jared's eyes were troubled. "I'm not a snitch."

"I don't think about it as you being a snitch. I think about it as you being smart," Brad replied. "And I know you're an intelligent guy, Jared."

Jared snorted. "Yeah, go tell my old man that."

Brad pushed back from the table. "I think we're done for now. Remember, if you think of anything that might be important, or you decide you want to come clean about everything, don't hesitate to contact your lawyer and I'll be available to you." There really wasn't much more he could say without coming off as a big phony, and that was the last thing he wanted Jared to think of him. Hopefully he'd built something with the kid, something that would pay off.

Minutes later Jared was led away by the jailer and Albright left the room. Brad could only wait and see if this short interview yielded anything.

There was no way Brad believed that the two teenagers hadn't talked about where they would go to hide out after the police were onto them for the murders. He believed Jared knew much more than he was telling.

Along with Leo, Jared had killed four men and Brad wished he would just confess to the murders. He could only hope the chat today had convinced Jared to come clean. Only time would tell.

It was possible Jared could be rehabilitated and eventually, at some point after serving years, he could get out of prison. Brad knew once Leo was captured, Jared's chances for that happening diminished. A judge might look more favorably on Jared if he confessed now and was truly remorseful for his actions.

Brad returned to his office, where he fielded some phone calls, coordinated with the officers working the case, and then when a lull occurred, he found himself thinking about his own father.

Certainly while Brad had never doubted his father's love for him, after the murder of Brad's mother, Brad had found himself having to take on the role of parent to his grieving father.

Before Brad's mother's death, Hank Howard had always appeared to be the strong one in the marriage, but Brad realized soon after his mother's death that Hank had depended on his wife a lot.

He'd had no idea about finances or how to shop or cook. He appeared helpless in the little things that held a family together. Brad had to step up and become the one who held his father together, who made sure things got done so they could function.

He hadn't minded, and not a day went by when his father didn't thank Brad for his strength. Not a day went by that his father didn't tell Brad that he was his hero.

Hank had never dated or thought about another relationship. He had loved his wife and had mourned for her all the rest of the days of his life. When he finally passed, Brad was happy only in the thought that his parents were united once again.

A knock fell on his door and Russ stuck his head into the office. "Simone Colton is here to see you," he said.

Brad frowned. What was she doing here? "Send her in," Brad said and ignored the googly eyes Russ made just before he closed the door.

A moment later the door opened and Simone stepped inside. She looked like a hot little firecracker in a red skirt and a red, white and blue blouse.

"Hey, I didn't expect to see you here today," he said as he got to his feet.

She smiled. "I stayed up last night and worked on a new profile for both Jared and Leo." She held out a sheath of papers, fastened together with a large blue paper clip. Her cheeks were dusted a charming shade of pink. "I hope you don't mind, but this was something I wanted to do and I hope you find it all useful."

"Thanks, Simone." He took the paperwork from her and laid it on his desk. "I'll be sure to read through it. How are you doing?"

"I'm good…just anxious for this all to come to an end," she replied.

"That makes two of us."

An awkward silence ensued, and then they both began speaking at the same time. They laughed and she took a step backward. "I know you're busy, so I'll get out of your hair now," she said. "I just wanted to drop off that paperwork. I don't know, but maybe it will help."

"Thank you. I appreciate it." He would have liked it if she lingered for a few minutes. But there was no reason for that to happen, and he needed to gain some distance from her.

He opened the door and she stepped out into the hallway. At the same time somebody yelled from the opposite end of the hall.

"Hey, stop. You have no right to barge in here," Russ's voice yelled.

"I'll barge in whenever I damned want to." At that moment Rob Garner appeared, barreling forward with Russ close behind him.

Garner's eyes widened and then narrowed at the sight of Simone. Oh, no, this was the last thing Brad wanted…another confrontation that put Simone in Rob's head.

"You," he snarled and pointed a finger at Simone. His hands balled into fists at his sides. "What in the hell are you doing here?" He didn't wait for an answer. "Was it your idea for my boy to be questioned without my presence? I warned you, lady. I warned you to keep your nose out of this. You're going to be damned sorry."

"I'm not going to stand here and listen to you threaten somebody," Brad said with a rising anger of his own. "If you want to speak with me, then have a seat in my office."

He turned to Simone. "Agent Dodd will see you out."

"This way, Miss Colton." Russ put himself between Simone and Garner. Garner stepped into Brad's office at the same time Russ disappeared down the hallway with Simone.

Brad remained in the hallway for several moments, tamping down the anger that threatened to consume him. Dammit, this was the very last thing he had needed. He'd seen the rage that had blackened Rob Garner's eyes as he'd confronted Simone. It was a rage that definitely concerned Brad for Simone's safety.

What was Garner really capable of? If he truly believed that Simone was somehow helping to put his son away, then how dangerous might he be to Simone?

Unfortunately, Brad didn't have the answer to that. Drawing a deep breath, he turned to go into his office to face Rob's wrath.

Simone added the finishing touches to her dining room table and then sank down to wait for her sisters and one of her cousins to arrive. It was rare that all three of them had a day off at the same time, but today they did and so she'd invited them all to lunch.

She'd ordered in chef salads and a light pasta salad as well. The food had already arrived, the table was set and she was eager to check in with Tatum and January. She'd also invited their cousin Carly and Simone was pleased that she was able to make it, too. The four girls had grown up together and Simone considered Carly like another sister.

It had been two days since she'd encountered Rob Garner at the police station. The more she saw of the man, the more she thought about what it must have been like for Jared to grow up with such a brutal man as a father.

She could feel sorry for the kid, but that certainly didn't excuse the choices he'd made, horrible choices that had resulted in four men being brutally murdered. When she thought about never seeing her father again, whatever Jared might have suffered as a kid didn't matter to her. He had still chosen to become a killer.

There was no question in her mind that Leo had been the dominant one in their friendship, that Leo had been the mastermind behind the murders. Leo was definitely a sociopath and he'd found the perfect partner in a boy who wanted to please and feel accepted by him.

A knock on the door pulled her out of her seat and out of her thoughts about Rob and Jared Garner. When she opened the door, Carly greeted her with a big hug.

"Come on in," Simone said. "You're the first to get here." She led Carly to the sofa, where they both sat. "How's work?" Simone asked.

"Good, but busy as usual." Carly was a pediatric nurse at Chicago University Hospital. "What about you?" Her bright blue eyes sparkled with interest.

"I've got a lecture tonight and then I'm finally all finished for the semester," Simone replied. "And how is Micha?"

Carly's eyes sparkled even brighter. "He's great."

Carly reached up and twirled a strand of her light blond hair. "Things are finally going really well and I couldn't be happier."

Carly had been engaged to Micha Harrison, a special forces army lieutenant. On his last mission he had been taken prisoner by a terrorist group out of Baghdad and Carly had gotten word that he was dead.

She had mourned long and deep for him and then a couple of months ago he'd walked back into her life. Scarred and having suffered a broken back, he'd decided it was better for him to let go of Carly so she could find another man to love, but he hadn't been able to stay away from her.

"I'm just glad Micha and I got a second chance together," Carly said.

Simone smiled. "And I'm so happy for both of you." Before she could say anything else, another knock sounded. It was Tatum and January.

Greetings and hugs were exchanged all around and then they all got seated at the table and began to catch up with each other. "I have a little confession to make," Tatum said. "I've started working on a cookbook."

"That's awesome," January exclaimed. "Are you going to publish it yourself? You know you could sell a lot of copies just by having it available in the restaurant."

"That's true, but I'd really like to find a publisher who could get me better distribution than just selling it out of the restaurant. So, keep your fingers crossed for me because I've been sending out some queries," Tatum replied.

She turned and looked at Simone. "What I really want to know from you is when Special Agent

Howard became Brad." She raised an eyebrow and both January and Carly looked at Simone quizzically.

"Oh, please, do tell," January said.

Simone's cheeks warmed. "Look, she's blushing," Carly exclaimed. "Simone, I swear, I have never seen you blush like that before."

"I'm not really blushing and there's nothing much to tell," Simone replied. "I… We… I've just been working with him a little bit."

"According to my staff, you looked pretty cozy at the restaurant before all hell broke loose," Tatum said.

"What happened? What hell broke loose?" January asked, looking first at Tatum and then at Simone.

Simone explained about approaching the Garners that night in the restaurant and how Rob had come at her. "He's a horrid man and he should have never become a father."

"Simone, you have to stay away from this," Tatum said. "I know you're just trying to help, but you just said yourself that Rob Garner is a horrid man. Who knows what he might be capable of?"

January reached out and took one of Simone's hands in hers. "The last thing we want is for anything to happen to you, Simone. In fact, we've been a little worried about you."

"Worried about me? Why?" Simone asked in surprise.

"You don't seem to be moving on," Tatum said softly. "It's been almost seven months now and you just seem completely obsessed."

"We don't want you anywhere near anything that might put you in danger."

"I know." Simone gave her sister's hand a squeeze and then released it. "In any case, that man would be a fool to come after me, especially now that he's threatened me in public twice."

"Twice?" Carly stared at her. "When did he threaten you the second time?"

Simone sighed. She hadn't intended to tell them about running into Rob at the police station, but inadvertently she had just busted herself. She told them about what had happened two days ago and listened to all three of them voice their concerns for her all over again.

"Don't worry. I don't expect to run into him again, and in any case, I think he's just a blowhard bully." What she didn't tell them was for the past two days as she'd run errands around town and in the neighborhood, she'd felt as if somehow somebody was following her...watching her, but she'd chalked it up to her own silly paranoia.

From that the conversation turned to how their mothers were doing and grilling Carly about what was happening with her two brothers.

The lunch lasted about an hour and a half. There was plenty of laughter, and by the time the others left, Simone was in a much better mood than she had been before they arrived.

Thank God she had her family. She wasn't sure how she would have survived this ordeal of loss without them. As she cleaned up the kitchen, thoughts of her father once again played through her mind.

She had definitely been a daddy's girl. Not only had he soothed her through stormy weather, he'd also been the one who had told her that the boy she'd liked in eighth grade was a jerk for not liking her back. He had taught her how to dance and how to drive a car. He'd also told her when her dress was too short and how to respect herself as a woman.

He had been the one man who had encouraged her drive and her thirst for knowledge. He'd been proud of who she had become and she'd loved to sit and talk to him for hours on end.

And now he was gone forever. The rock concert of grief suddenly screamed in her head. She hoped Brad was right and in time her grief would only be a whisper of a lullaby that occasionally played in her head.

Brad. The man was spending far too much time in her head. Of all the men in Chicago, why did it have to be a handsome FBI agent from Washington, DC, who drew her in?

She enjoyed watching the ever-changing colors of his hazel eyes…from green to gold to goldish brown. Why did his broad shoulders and strong arms beckon her to fall into them and just be for a moment? Why did she enjoy talking to him more than she had to any other man?

It was wrong…all wrong, and she knew it. He had a job to do here, and once that job was over, he'd return to whatever life he had in DC. Besides, he was probably just being kind to her because she was the daughter of a victim and because she'd pretty much been in his face for the last week or two.

Or maybe she was just thinking about him so much because he was a distraction from her grief. Certainly it was easier for her to think about the handsome FBI agent than to think about her father's forever absence from her life.

She just had to stop thinking about him altogether now. He would contact her and the rest of her family if anything changed with the case. She'd done what she could to help and now there was no reason for her to spend any time alone again with Brad.

After the kitchen was once again clean, she sat down at the table with her notes for the night's lecture before her and read through them. She'd been there for only about a half an hour when rain began to patter against the window.

She got up and turned on her television in an effort to catch the weather report for the evening. The forecast wasn't great. It was supposed to rain all night and through tomorrow. There was no way she'd be walking to the college tonight. She definitely wasn't into walking in the rain no matter how big the umbrella she carried.

By six thirty she was in her car and headed to the campus. The rain had continued to come down steadily throughout the afternoon and it had turned unusually cool.

As much as she loved the students she would be teaching tonight, she was eager to get back to her condo, change into her nightgown and cuddle down beneath a soft, warm blanket.

She parked in the staff parking lot, opened her umbrella and grabbed her computer case and then hurried toward the lecture hall for the last time until next fall. Once again, she had that odd feeling of somebody watching her. She threw a glance over her shoulder but saw nobody anywhere near her.

Still, she breathed a small sigh of relief as she entered the building. She closed the umbrella and smiled at the security guard who stood just inside the door. "It's a wet one out there tonight, Eddie," she said.

Eddie Judd had worked security for as long as she could remember. He was a really nice older guy who had retired from the police department and then had picked up the job working security.

"Supposed to be wet for the next week or so," Eddie replied. "Have a good evening, Professor Colton."

"Thanks, Eddie. You do the same." She hurried down the carpeted hallway toward the lecture room that held two hundred students, although the class tonight wasn't that big.

Once inside, she went to the lectern, prepared her notes, connected her computer to the audio/ video system and then greeted the students as they began to trickle in. Once seven o'clock came, the hall was three-quarters of the way full and she began her lecture, complete with an elaborate PowerPoint presentation.

As always, the students were quiet and attentive until around eight o'clock when she asked for questions. They were a lively bunch and for the next half an hour they not only asked questions of her, but also challenged each other with opinions and theories.

At just after eight thirty she closed by telling them all goodbye for the summer. It took another fifteen minutes or so for the hall to empty and for her to pack away her notes and computer and then prepare to leave the building.

"Good night, Eddie. I hope you have a great summer," she said as she approached the door.

"Back at you, Professor Colton," the older man replied. "Try to stay dry."

"You do the same," she replied.

It was still raining when she stepped back outside with her keys and umbrella in one hand and her computer case in the other. She hurried toward her car parked in the staff parking area as the rain thrummed a tune on the umbrella material over her head.

She was almost to her car when she heard a slapping of footsteps on the pavement behind her. Her heartbeat accelerated and she half turned but was suddenly struck hard in the back by somebody.

She cried out and stumbled, but before she could regain her balance, she was pulled backward by a viscous yank on her hair. She pressed the alarm button on her car and heard it begin to shrilly beep and then she was falling…falling backward.

She gasped in excruciating pain as the back of her head crashed into the concrete. For a brief moment myriad stars danced in her head and then the stars dissolved and there was nothing but darkness.

Leo curled up beneath the tent under the highway overpass and watched the rain pour down. There was a little tent city in this spot. Homeless people and drug addicts were his neighbors, although he certainly hadn't interacted with them.

He was good for now. He'd found enough to eat

in a garbage dumpster behind a food store. His phone was fully charged thanks to a charging station at a truck stop and he'd managed to dye his dark brown hair a funky red that he hoped would keep the feds off his back.

He'd ditched his signature chain and lock that he was known for wearing as well as the camo clothing that might help somebody identify him. He'd also stolen a kid's skateboard. Now he looked like just one more of the skateboard kids who ran the streets. He hated it. He deserved so much better than this.

If only Jared hadn't gotten caught. The stupid jerk hadn't even been able to get out of his own way the night the FBI crashed in. Now Jared was in jail and it probably wouldn't be long before he'd not only confess to the four murders, but he'd also try to throw Leo under the bus.

Rob Garner had convinced Leo that he was keeping his son strong and not talking, but for how long? Unfortunately, when Leo had jumped out of the window to escape that night, he'd had to leave his bug-out bag with all his cash behind. And now his own parents weren't helping him at all. They had basically disowned him. It would serve them right if he broke into the house in the middle of the night and slashed their throats.

All he needed was enough money to get out of town until things cooled down and then eventually he might be able to get out of the country. All he needed was somebody to give him a freakin' break.

At that moment his phone rang. It was a burner phone and he knew exactly who was on the other end. "Yeah," he answered.

"Something has to be done about that Colton bitch. She's going to somehow burn you both."

"So, what do you want me to do about it?" Leo asked. Bingo. This was definitely his freakin' break.

"She needs to disappear…permanently. I tried to take care of the situation tonight, but I'm not sure it worked."

"Again, what do you want me to do about it?" Leo repeated. Rob Garner wasn't a stupid man. He knew it was in Jared's best interest if Leo was never brought in.

Although Leo wasn't sure if Rob truly knew how bad it would be for his son. Leo wouldn't have a problem throwing Jared under the bus. He would get all choked up while he told a jury how Jared had manipulated him into shooting the gun and killing those men. He'd sob nearly uncontrollably as he told them he had feared for his own life with Jared and his father's threats.

"She's tight with that FBI agent, Howard. It wouldn't hurt if something bad happened to both of them. It would probably slow down the case and give us more of a chance at a really good defense," Rob continued.

For the first time since he'd shot those old men outside their businesses, a fresh, sweet adrenaline rushed through Leo. "So, tell me exactly what you have in mind."

Chapter 5

It was a few minutes after ten and Brad was ready to call it another failure of a day. Styler was still out there. Rob Garner was still bitching and moaning about Jared now being questioned without him present and about everything else concerning the case against his son. And Brad hadn't seen or spoken to Simone in two days.

As it should be, he reminded himself. He'd read over the notes she'd given to him and marveled at her insights. If the notes were any indication of how she taught, then he could understand why her classes were so popular. She had a way of laying out information that made it easy to understand, yet her intelligence in the subject matter shone through.

However, at this point there was nothing more she could do to help and the two of them had absolutely no reason to get together again. In fact, as far as he was concerned, it would be utter foolishness for him to pursue anything with Simone Colton.

He had just undressed and crawled into bed when a knock sounded at his door. He jumped up, hoping it was somebody telling him they'd finally caught Leo.

He yanked on a pair of jeans, grabbed his gun and then answered the door. It was Russ. "Hey, I just got word from a Chicago PD friend of mine that your girl has been taken by ambulance to Chicago University Hospital."

His girl? Simone? "What? Did he know why?" Every muscle in Brad's body tensed as his mind went wild with worry.

"He didn't have any real details, but he thought it was something about a carjacking." Russ frowned. "I figured you'd want to know. Do you want me to go with you?"

"No... I'm fine to go." Brad grabbed the shirt that he'd worn that day and pulled it on. "You get some sleep and I'll be in touch tomorrow."

When Russ left the room, Brad quickly got on his socks and shoes. A carjacking? She had to have been hurt to be taken to the hospital. Oh God, had she been badly hurt? All kinds of crazy thoughts rushed through his head, only making him more anxious and eager to get to her as soon as possible.

A few minutes later he left the hotel room and headed for the police-issued unmarked car that had been at his disposal since he had arrived in Chicago. Rain fell at a moderate pace, as it had all evening long.

As he drove to the hospital, his brain continued to go wild with suppositions. Had a gun been involved? Had she been shot? Or had this been something much more dangerous…much more insidious than a carjacking?

Rob Garner. A vision of the man angrily threatening Simone filled his head. Did he have something to do with Simone being in the hospital? Or was Brad overthinking things? There was plenty of crime on the Chicago streets without Rob Garner being in the mix.

Right now he didn't care so much about answering these questions. All he really cared about was her condition. It seemed like it took him forever to reach the hospital. Traffic was slow and people drove like they had never driven in the rain before. He found a parking space in the hospital lot and then raced for the emergency room.

The waiting area was half filled with people. A little boy fussed and cried in his mother's arms and an old man had one hand wrapped in a makeshift bandage. A young couple sat side by side, her head resting on his shoulder. Two young women paced the floor, looking sick and strung out.

A hospital was definitely not Brad's favorite place to be. His mother had lingered three long days before succumbing to the wounds from her killer. Brad's father had brought him to visit every day.

He'd been convinced that Brad's mother would rally, that she would somehow be okay, but Brad had smelled the death in the room, had seen the shadow of death on his mother's face and had known even at twelve years old that she wasn't going to have a miraculous healing.

He now went to the desk, where a harried-looking nurse sat behind a glass partition. He flashed his credentials and she opened the window. "Can I help you?"

"A woman named Simone Colton was brought in here by ambulance about an hour ago. I need to speak to the doctor in charge of her case."

"Please, have a seat and I'll see what I can do," she replied.

With a sigh of frustration, he sank down in a chair near the window. He waited ten minutes and then finally the nurse waved at him and opened the door that separated the waiting room from the curtained-off emergency beds.

Brad hurried through the door and was met by a young doctor who wore the name tag of Dr. McCoy.

Once again, Brad showed his credentials and then enquired about Simone.

"Miss Colton was brought in after having suffered a head trauma that rendered her unconscious. She regained consciousness soon after arriving. We've now run the appropriate tests to make sure she didn't have a fracture or any brain bleed. Both tests came back negative, but I've had her transferred to a bed upstairs for a night of observation."

"What room has she been transferred to and can I see her?" Brad asked, his emotions flying all over the place. He needed to know how she had ended up here with head trauma.

"She's in room 605. I'll tell you what I told the officers that came in with her. I don't want her stressed by too many questions. The main thing she needs right now is rest."

"Got it," Brad replied and hurried back to the exit of the waiting room. Once there he went down a long hallway and came to the elevators that would take him up to the sixth floor.

His heart thundered in his chest. She'd suffered a head trauma… What did that even mean? Had somebody tried to jack her car and hit her over the head with the butt of a gun? With a crowbar? Where had this happened? He didn't even know what kind of a car she drove.

Once the elevator doors whooshed open, he quickly stepped out, checked the sign on the wall and then raced in the direction of her room. The halls were quiet and the lights were dimmed at this time of the night.

He was vaguely surprised when he reached her room to find nobody else there with her. She lay in the bed, a lamp just above her head casting light on her pale face. Her eyes were closed and she looked small and achingly vulnerable in the big hospital bed.

He needed to contact somebody. He needed answers as to what had happened to her, but at the moment he just needed to stand in the doorway and watch the steady rise and fall of her chest beneath her blue-flowered hospital gown. He needed to gaze at her beautiful face and assure himself that, at least for now, she seemed to be safe and resting peacefully.

Suddenly he was gazing into her bright blue eyes. "Simone," he whispered softly.

Her eyes widened. She looked around the room and then back at him and then a deep sob escaped her and she raised her hands to hide her face.

"Simone…" In four long strides he was at her bedside. "Please don't cry," he said.

"I…I can't h-help it, Brad. I was so…so scared and m-my head is k-killing me."

He sank down next to her in a chair. "Simone, crying is only going to make your head hurt more. You're safe now." He reached out and pulled one of her hands away from her face. He held on tight and slowly she lowered her other hand and gazed at him through tear-filled eyes.

He continued to hold her hand as she drew in a few deep breaths in an obvious effort to calm herself. For several moments they were silent. Although there were a hundred questions he wanted to ask her, he also wanted to give her enough time to gather herself together.

Finally, her tears stopped and her eyes were more clear. "Simone, I don't want to upset you, but I need to know what happened tonight."

She reached for a water cup on a small tray on the opposite side of the bed. She took a swallow, then set down the foam cup. "I...I had my last lecture tonight. It all went great and afterward I headed for my car in the staff parking lot." She paused and a whisper of fear darkened her eyes.

"It was raining and I...I was almost to my car," she continued, "when I heard a couple of footsteps behind me. I started to turn and then I was shoved hard and my hair was yanked. Somehow, I managed to push my car alarm before I fell backward and hit the concrete with my head. I woke up here. The doctor told me the two police officers who followed the ambulance believed it was a carjacking gone awry."

She winced slightly and then pulled the thin hospital blanket up closer around her neck. "To be honest, I don't know what to believe. It all happened so fast. I suppose it might have been a carjacking. I can't imagine what else it would have been."

"Were there other cars in that parking lot?" he asked.

She nodded and then winced again, her headache obviously causing her pain. "There were a few."

He asked her several more questions and he could tell she grew more and more weary.

She drew in a deep, heavy sigh. "Brad, I don't want any of my family knowing about this. I'll be out of the hospital tomorrow and there's no need to worry any of them."

"I will do my best not to tell anyone," he replied. "Now, the best thing you can do is get a good night's sleep." He rose from the chair.

The instinct…the need to lean down and kiss her on the forehead or on her cheek shocked him. Instead, he quickly stepped back from the bed. "I'll be back in the morning, Simone."

"Thank you, Brad." Her eyes slowly drifted closed and he stepped outside of the room. He hurried down the hallway a little ways and then pulled his cell phone from his pocket. He was far enough away that she wouldn't be able to hear his conversation, but close enough that he still had his eye on her room.

He needed to speak to the officers who had responded to the scene, but first he needed to call the lieutenant who was the liaison between the FBI agents and the Chicago PD. He wanted to arrange for a guard on Simone's door.

Even though the police had believed it was a carjacking, Brad's gut instincts told him that there was a real possibility it might be something different. It was just too coincidental that Rob had threatened her and then she was attacked in a staff parking lot.

There was no way to be sure his instincts were right or wrong, but he wasn't taking any chances with Simone's safety. It took forty-five minutes for a police officer to show up for the guard duty. He settled into a chair in the doorway of her room and told Brad he would be there until Brad returned the next morning.

The next place Brad went was to the police station to see if he could hunt down the two officers who had responded to the 911 call made by a security guard at the college. He got lucky and found both of them together at their desks.

They agreed to meet with him in one of the interrogation rooms that currently wasn't in use. "I just want to get the rundown on what happened when you arrived at the call on the campus earlier."

Mike Walker was a young patrolman. He frowned. "When my partner and I arrived on scene, Miss Colton was unconscious on the ground. Her car alarm was going off, which had alerted the security guard who called it in."

"I immediately checked the area for a perp, but I didn't see anyone around." Paul Winthrop appeared to be the older, the more seasoned of the two.

"Where were her car keys?" Brad asked.

"In her hand," Mike replied. "Although her computer case and an umbrella were on the ground near her. It looked like an open-and-shut case to me."

"If she was unconscious with her keys in her hand, then why wasn't her car stolen?" Brad asked.

"It would be my speculation that the alarm scared the carjacker off," Paul said.

"Do you know how long the alarm rang before the security guard responded?" Brad asked.

"He wasn't sure. He only heard it when he stepped outside to have a smoke. Do you know how she's doing? She was still unconscious when we were with her earlier," Mike said.

"I just left the hospital and she's going to be okay. She's being held overnight for observation, but she should be out of the hospital sometime tomorrow," Brad explained.

"That's good to hear," Paul replied.

"Can you email me your reports when you get them written up?" Brad asked.

"I've already written mine up," Paul replied. "Just give me your email and it will be done."

Brad gave the two men his email address and then thanked them. When they parted ways, Brad's impulse was to rush back to the hospital, but he knew he had other things to do in order to assure Simone's safety going forward.

He went back to his office and read Paul's report and then just sat for several minutes trying to clear his mind. He needed to think rationally and not emotionally.

It was evident that everyone he had spoken to believed it had been a carjacking gone awry, but all his instincts screamed it had been Rob or somebody close to Rob who had attacked her.

He'd seen the hatred in the man's eyes both times he'd encountered Simone. Worse than the hatred had been the whisper of fear he'd seen in Rob's eyes.

Brad believed Rob saw Simone as a viable threat to Jared's freedom, and if that was the case, then he was a clear and present danger to her. If what Brad believed was true, then tonight Rob had attacked her. The car alarm very well might have saved her life.

If Rob's intention had been to take her out permanently, then tonight he had failed. What scared Brad was that meant another attack was possible, and the next time Rob just might succeed.

Simone awakened with the morning light drifting in through the blinds at the window. For a moment she was disoriented. Then the memories of the night before slammed into her.

Her headache had finally abated, but she now felt more aches and pains in her back from hitting the concrete. As she thought of the sudden, violent attack, a chill swept through her. Everything had happened so fast and she desperately wished she had seen her attacker so that the police would have a physical description of whoever it had been.

Unfortunately, because it had all happened so fast and she'd been attacked from behind, she hadn't seen the person. The police had been certain that it had been a carjacking. For as long as she had worked at the college, she'd never heard of any carjackings occurring there. But she supposed it was possible that was what it had been. There was really no other scenario that made any sense.

A vision of an enraged Rob Garner filled her head. She still didn't believe she needed to take his threats seriously, and she didn't think he had anything to do with what had happened to her the night before. But what if she was wrong? She didn't want to believe that it was anything other than a random act of violence. To believe that Rob Garner had been behind the attack was just too frightening to consider.

Her thoughts turned to Brad. Thoughts of him always made her heart flutter just a bit. There was no question that she felt a strong physical attraction toward him, but what woman wouldn't? He was definitely easy on the eyes. While she had found him easy to talk to, there was no way there would be anything between them except the murder that had temporarily brought them together.

Her thoughts were interrupted by the appearance of a nurse, who took her vitals and pronounced all of them good. "The doctor will be in soon," she said and then left the room.

It wasn't the doctor who came in next, though. It was breakfast. She ate the toast and drank both the orange juice and coffee but didn't have the appetite for the scrambled eggs or the limp bacon. She pushed the tray away and then settled back into her pillow.

She didn't realize she'd fallen back asleep, but when she opened her eyes, Brad was seated in the chair next to her bed. "Oh my gosh, how long have you been there?" she asked and raised up the head of her bed.

"Not too long. How are you feeling?"

He looked great in a pair of jeans and a navy polo shirt. As usual, a shoulder holster with his gun was his only accessory. Her hand self-consciously went up to her hair and then dropped back to her lap. She had no idea what she looked like at the moment, but in the end it really didn't matter.

"My headache is better, but I've definitely discovered some new body aches and pains today," she replied.

"I'm not surprised. You took a hard fall last

night." His gaze was warm and intense as it lingered on her. "When I got the call that you'd been taken to the hospital, it scared the hell out of me."

"I have to confess, when I woke up in the hospital, I was pretty scared myself. I just wish I could have given the police officers a description of the person or persons so they could get him…or them off the streets."

"There's no question things would be different if you had seen who attacked you. However, I'm not convinced what happened to you was a carjacking."

She stared at him. "You think it was Rob Garner?"

"I do." A muscle throbbed in his lower jaw. "I warned you to stay away from him."

She picked up on a bit of frustrated anger in his voice and it stirred a touch of defensive anger in her. "I'll admit I made a mistake when I approached him in the restaurant, but it wasn't my fault that we ran into each other in the police station when I brought you my notes."

For a long moment their gazes remained locked. Finally, he raked a hand through his short hair and released a deep sigh. "Sorry, I'm not angry with you. I'm just angered by this whole situation."

"I'm not exactly happy about it, either," she replied drily.

At that moment a doctor entered the room. He

introduced himself as Dr. Matt Jacobs. "How are you feeling this morning, Miss Colton?"

"Make it Simone and I'm feeling much better. Please tell me I can go home."

"Only if you promise that if your headache returns or if you suffer any dizziness or unusual drowsiness, you'll either follow up with your doctor or return to the emergency room," he replied.

"I promise," she said.

"Then I'll have the nurse work up your discharge papers."

"Thank you, Dr. Jacobs."

"Would you please step out so I can get dressed?" Simone asked Brad once the doctor left the room.

"Of course," Brad replied. He immediately stood and headed for the doorway.

Simone got up and checked the closet, where she found the clothes she'd had on the night before hanging there. Her purse and her computer case were also there. She assumed one of the officers had sent them along with her in the ambulance. She dressed quickly and then went to the door to let Brad know he could come back in.

She was surprised to see him speaking to a police officer who was seated in a chair just outside her room. She stepped back before either man saw her and instead she sat on the edge of her bed to wait for Brad and her discharge papers.

He knocked on the door and she told him to

come in. When he entered the room again, she looked at him curiously. "Who is the officer in the chair?"

"His name is Officer Eric Mendez. I had him sit on guard duty outside your room all night long."

"Did you really think that was necessary?" she asked. Her heart began to beat a little bit faster. She suddenly felt as if her orderly life was spinning out of control and she didn't like the feeling at all.

"I would prefer to err on the side of safety," he replied. "And with that in mind, I hope you don't mind but I've called your sisters to meet me and you at your place at two o'clock this afternoon." He once again sat in the chair next to the bed.

She stared at him for a long moment. "Did you tell them what happened to me?"

He hesitated a moment and then looked away. "Yeah, I did."

Another edge of anger rose up inside her. "I asked you not to tell them."

He looked back at her and there was a hard glint in his eyes. "Simone, I am first and foremost an FBI agent, and I thought it was in everyone's best interest to know what happened to you last night."

"But why? It could only have been one of two things. Either it was a random act or it was Rob Garner. In either case, why did they have to know anything?"

"I'll explain more about it when we're all together with your sisters," he replied. "I'll take you home and we'll wait for them there."

"Where is my car? Is it still at the college?" She was trying not to be upset, but once again she felt as if her carefully structured world was turning upside down.

"I arranged for your car to be taken back to your condo parking spot." He stood and reached into his pocket. He pulled out her key fob and held it out to her. She took it from him and dropped it into her purse.

An awkward silence ensued. She knew Brad wasn't telling her something and that worried her. What was going on that he felt the need to involve her family at all? She refused to beg him for the answers right now, but she couldn't help the nerves that jangled inside her.

Thankfully the nurse walked in at that moment with her discharge paperwork, breaking the sudden tension that had risen up between them.

Once Simone was free to go, she and Brad left the hospital and he led her to his car. Since he'd flown into Chicago, she knew the car wasn't his personal one, but rather one the Chicago PD had loaned him for the duration of his time here.

The brief sunshine of the morning was gone and rain had moved in again. Unfortunately, her umbrella hadn't been with her clothes and purse, so they raced to get to the car. Once there, Brad quickly opened the car door for her and she slid inside.

The car interior smelled like Brad's cologne, and even with everything that was going on, her stomach tightened with what only could be described as a faint hint of sexual tension. Or was it simply anxiety? Because she knew something was about to happen and she had no idea if that something was going to be good or very, very bad.

Chapter 6

Brad knew instinctively that Simone wasn't going to be happy with his plans for her, but he would do anything he needed to do to keep her safe from harm.

Still, he could already feel her tension radiating toward him in the car. It felt very negative and as if she'd closed herself off.

"Headache still gone?" he asked in an effort to break the uncomfortable silence that had grown between them.

"Yes, thank goodness," she replied. "Last night I could scarcely think it pounded so hard."

"I'm glad you're feeling better today." He flashed her a smile, hoping to break the tension.

"I'm just glad I'm finished up with all my

classes. I'll also just be glad to get home and relax for the next few days."

Brad didn't reply because that wasn't at all what he had in mind for her. Again silence fell between them until he pulled up in a parking space across from her condo. Thankfully the rain had stopped, but the skies were still dark gray.

She released what sounded like a sigh of relief. "Oh, it's good to be here instead of the hospital," she said as they got out of the car. "The first thing I want to do is take a nice, long hot shower."

Instantly a vision of her naked and beneath the shower spray filled his head. He could imagine the soap sliding down her body… The scent of her filled his head and a rush of heat took over his body.

Jeez, what was wrong with him? Where was his professionalism when he needed it? How could he be thinking of her in that way when it was possible her life was in danger? He gave himself a hard mental shake.

As she unlocked the door to the condo, he was interested in what her home looked like. You could tell a lot about a person by the things they chose to have around them.

She opened the door and ushered him into an attractive living room. The floor plan was open and airy. Pictures of her siblings and parents covered one wall. It was proof that the person who lived here had strong family ties.

The color combinations were relaxing and the overstuffed sofa looked inviting. The whole space felt warm. He could also tell there was a place for everything and everything was in its place, whispering of a bit of a control issue? Or just a person who was well organized?

"It's after noon. Do you want me to make you something for lunch?" she offered.

"No, thanks, I'm good. Why don't you go ahead and take that shower you wanted," he replied.

She gave him a grateful smile. "Thanks. I'll be back in a few minutes."

"Take your time." As she disappeared from the room, he stepped over to the wall of photos. He couldn't help the way his heart responded to the pictures of Alfred with his wife and three daughters. His murder had been so senseless and now there would never be a family photo with all of them present in it again.

As he heard the water turn on in the bathroom, he sat down on the sofa and went over the plans he had made the night before. He'd been up all night making sure his plans were in place and everything was taken care of.

It was really perfect, but he had a feeling Simone was going to kick and buck, which was why he'd invited her sisters to be here for backup and support.

He hadn't gone into much detail when he'd spoken to each of them, but his instinct in this matter was that they were definitely going to be on his side. He hoped Simone would be reasonable and realize she needed to do what was necessary.

Twenty minutes later Simone walked back out. She looked amazing in a pair of jeans that hugged the slender length of her long legs and a blue-and-white sleeveless blouse that emphasized the thrust of her breasts and her small waist.

She smelled like clean female with a hint of the perfume that made him think of snuggling and hot sex. Criminy, this was going to be the most difficult thing he had ever done in his entire career.

"Are you sure you aren't hungry?" she asked. "I'd be glad to make you a sandwich or something while we wait for my sisters to get here."

"Yes, I'm sure, but feel free to make yourself something if you're hungry."

"I'm not," she replied and sank down in the chair facing him. "Brad, I'm sorry you've had to deal with all this. I'm sure there are far more important things you should be doing with your time right now."

"Actually, there isn't. I've got a good team and they all know what we need to do. Of course, the main goal is to get Leo behind bars."

She frowned. "Do you think he's somehow managed to get out of the country?"

"No. I don't even think he's made it out of Chicago. My guess is that he's hunkered down someplace and is waiting for the heat to ease off him before he'll make a move."

"But how is he existing? His parents have to somehow be getting money to him," she said.

"If they are, we can't figure out how. We have eyes on all their financials and nothing suspicious has shown up. We also have tails on them, but again they haven't done anything to indicate they have aided Leo. They've told us they've washed their hands of him and have no desire to help their son given the crimes he will be charged with."

She released a deep sigh and then leaned back in the chair. "So, you want to tell me now why you've invited my sisters to meet us here?"

"I'll wait until we're all here together. It won't be long before they'll be here," he replied.

"You're driving me crazy with your mysteriousness."

He smiled at her. "Normally I'm not mysterious at all. I'm pretty much an open book kind of guy."

She returned his smile. "Brad, I just want to thank you for everything you've done. Not just for me, but for my entire family."

"I'm just doing my job," he replied.

"Being at the hospital to take me home was certainly going above and beyond your job," she replied.

"Simone, you're a party of interest in an ongoing investigation. What happens with you *is* part of my job," he replied. And he needed to keep reminding himself that he was just doing his job and it had nothing to do with his intense, inexplicable attraction to Simone.

For the next few minutes, they talked about the case and threw out speculations on where Leo might be hiding. At precisely two o'clock, their conversation was interrupted by a knock at the door.

"I'll get it," Brad said and quickly jumped up from the sofa. With his hand on the butt of his gun, he opened the door. He relaxed at the sight of Tatum. She greeted him and then quickly beelined to Simone.

She grabbed Simone's hand and pulled her up off the chair and into a big hug. "Oh my God, Simone. Are you okay? I couldn't believe it when Agent Howard told me what happened to you last night."

"I'm fine," Simone assured her. "I've just got a little bump on the back of my head." She returned to her seat and gestured for Tatum to sit on the sofa.

"I've got a million questions to ask you about exactly what happened, but I'll wait until January gets here because I know she'll have the same questions I have." The words had barely left Tatum's mouth when another knock sounded at the door.

January flew through the door and more hugs were given. Finally, everyone was settled in. The two sisters and Brad on the sofa and Simone in the chair.

After a fifteen-minute session of asking Simone for all the details concerning exactly what had happened to her the night before and Simone answering all the questions, they then looked expectantly to Brad.

He cleared his throat and stood. "I'm sure you all are wondering why I've brought you together. Now that you know what happened to Simone last night, I have to tell you I don't believe it was a carjacking or a random attack."

"Then who do you think attacked her?" Tatum asked.

"All my instincts tell me it was Rob Garner, or somebody working with him," Brad replied.

"Why would Jared Garner's father be after Simone? What would he have to gain by attacking her?" Tatum stared at Simone and then looked back to Brad. "We know about the two encounters she had with the man, but do you really believe he'd follow through with physical violence?"

"This is what I think," Brad said. "I believe Rob now believes that Simone is actively working to see his son put away in prison forever. I believe he sees her as a danger to his family, and because of that, he's a real danger to Simone. I think he tried to kill her last night and was unsuccessful. I think he'll try again. My plan is to get Simone out of town and hidden away until either Jared confesses or Leo is captured."

"Oh, no," Simone instantly said. She halfway rose from the chair and then sat back down again. "I'm not leaving my home because of this big-mouthed bully."

"Simone, he's more than a bully. Even you know that he beats his son. He's a brutal man and I believe he'll come after you again," Brad said firmly.

"Then you have to go, Simone," Tatum said firmly.

"Simone, there's no question about it. You must go," January added. "We can't take any risks with your safety. I refuse to lose another family member. Mom would want you to go, too."

"I think you're all overreacting," Simone said, her slightly narrowed eyes telling Brad she was irritated with him.

"But what if I'm not?" Brad replied. The whole situation had burned in his gut all night long. He'd tried to make himself believe that the attack on her had been random and had nothing to do with Rob Garner, but he'd been unsuccessful.

He truly believed he needed to get her away from Chicago and he'd made the perfect arrangements. The only thing he needed to do now was convince her to go with him.

"Simone, you have no work to worry about right now. You have nothing on your plate that is more important than your very life," Tatum said.

Simone looked at both her sisters and then released an audible deep sigh. She looked back at Brad. "Okay. What do you have in mind?"

"My buddy has a small fishing cabin about five hours from here. Nobody will know we're there and I can keep you safe ."

She frowned. "Do we really need to do this?"

"Yes," both of her sisters exclaimed at the same time.

Simone looked at Brad once again. "When would we have to leave?"

"Immediately. I already have my bags packed and in the car. All you need to do is pack whatever you need for a week or two and then we'll get on the road," he replied.

Tatum got up from the sofa and grabbed Simone's hand. "Come on, I'll help you pack."

"You'll keep her safe?" January asked him as the other two left the room.

"I'll die before I let anything happen to her," he replied with all the determination in his heart, in his very soul.

January held his gaze for a long moment and then nodded, as if satisfied. It was true. He would protect Simone with his life, not just because it was his job, but also because it was his desire. He couldn't imagine anyone hurting her and it wouldn't happen on his watch. The Colton families had already endured enough.

"Let me go see how they're doing," January said

and then disappeared into the room where the other two had gone.

Brad walked over to the window that looked out onto the street. He was eager to get on the road, but before they left town, they needed to stop by a grocery store and get food and anything else they might need for the next couple of weeks.

If he remembered right, Glen's cabin was fairly isolated and there was just a very small general store a few miles away. The store sold only the very basics but had a large supply of alcohol.

Rain had begun to fall again from the gray clouds above. He hadn't heard any weather reports in the last couple of days, but he was definitely hoping the clouds would break up and the rain would stop once they got underway.

He'd received permission from his superior to get Simone out of town. There were only a few people at the police station who knew where he was taking Simone. He definitely hoped there would be no leaks that might let the Garners, or anyone else nefarious, know where they had gone.

He turned around from the window when the three women returned to the room. Simone carried one medium-sized suitcase and Tatum had a smaller one.

"All set?" Brad asked.

"Not really," Simone replied. "I'm not happy about any of this."

"Simone, I'd rather have you unhappy and safe than happy and dead," Tatum said. "Go with Agent Howard and don't be stubborn about things."

"You need to listen to him and do everything he tells you to do," January added. "We'll explain all of this to Mom."

"Let's get on the road," Brad said.

He took her bags and they left the condo. The sisters all hugged and said their goodbyes and then it was just him and Simone in the car and he pulled away from her condo.

"Well, that was certainly quite manipulative of you, Agent Howard," she said coolly.

He shot her a look of surprise. "What are you talking about?" he asked.

"Planning ahead to have my sisters there to coerce me into coming with you. It was a really sneaky thing to do."

"Okay, I'll admit it was a little manipulative, but I just wanted to make sure you came with me. As far as I'm concerned, this is a matter of life or death and I would do it all over again for this intended result."

"I much would have preferred if you had approached me on an intellectual level rather than on an emotional one," she said, her voice still decidedly cool. "If I were a man, would you have had my two brothers waiting to talk me into coming with you?"

"It would depend on how stubborn you were as a man," he said in an attempt at levity. It didn't work. Without even looking at her, he felt the weight of her baleful stare.

He released a deep sigh. They were about to be alone for a week or two in an isolated cabin by a river in the woods. He hoped she managed to forgive him soon. Otherwise, rather than being a hideaway of protection, it would wind up being the hideaway from hell.

The foul mood had Simone around the throat and she was having trouble climbing out of it. There was no question that she was irritated with Brad for involving her family members in her drama, but she could admit to herself that she probably wouldn't have agreed to come without her sisters' insistence.

However, her real irritation was at the whole situation, at the fact that she was now in a car heading to a cabin in the woods because some psychopath decided she was a danger to him and his family. Her well-structured life was now no longer in her control and she felt as if her world had been tossed on its head.

"There's a grocery store a couple of blocks from here," he said. "We'll stop there to shop for food to take with us. I've got a cooler in the trunk full of ice for the trip."

"Sounds like you've thought of everything," she

replied. Good grief, even to herself she sounded cranky.

"I've tried to," he replied, as if oblivious of her current mood.

Minutes later they entered the grocery store and she walked beside him as he pushed the cart. As they shopped, she felt her bad mood slowly lifting.

Even though she didn't want to be here, she needed to make the best of things. Just as it really wasn't her fault that Rob Garner had a problem with her, it wasn't Brad's fault, either. He was just trying to keep her safe and that was what she needed to remember.

They passed an aisle with candy bars and she grabbed a chocolate bar and tossed it into the cart. "Chocolate makes me less witchy," she said and then laughed when Brad grabbed a handful and added them to the cart.

Forty-five minutes later they were back in the car. "I think we bought enough groceries to last a month," she said as he pulled out of the grocery store parking lot.

"I'm sure we won't be gone that long, but I like to be prepared," he replied.

"Could you please do something about this rain?" she asked as the wipers worked overtime to keep the car window clean.

"Ha, wish I could. Hopefully it will stop soon or we'll eventually drive out of it."

"So, tell me about this cabin we're going to."

"Glen Tankersley works as a police officer in a small town in Wisconsin. I met him while investigating a serial killer that was working there and we became good friends. He's a fishing freak and years ago bought a cabin that's on the bank of a small river. He did tell me it's been a while since he'd been there."

"You still haven't told me about the cabin itself," she replied. She looked at him, unable to ignore his handsome profile.

"It's been years since I've been there, but it's a one-bedroom with pretty much everything you need. It has a stove and fridge, a wood-burning fireplace and a bathroom. Unfortunately, there's no tub, just a shower. I remember it as a cozy little getaway."

"Sounds like the perfect hideaway," she agreed and then looked back out her passenger window. A one-bedroom cabin. Did he assume that they would sleep together in the bed?

And why did the very idea shoot a tiny whisper of a thrill through her? It was going to be difficult to share a small space with him and stay as completely distant from him as she knew she should.

Still, she couldn't remember ever feeling the kind of physical attraction that she felt toward Brad for any other man. She had to keep reminding herself that he was just doing his job, and when his job was finished, he'd go back to his life in Washington, DC.

The windshield wipers beat in a rhythmic manner that, along with the grayness of the day, slowly relaxed her. Oddly enough she hadn't felt any danger, but right now in this moment with Brad taking control, she felt completely safe and protected. She closed her eyes and let the movement of the car and the patter of the rain against the window lull her to sleep.

She awakened to the darkness of night and the windshield wipers still working overtime. "Wow, how long have I been asleep?"

"About four and a half hours. We're pretty close to the cabin now," he replied.

"I'm so sorry. I certainly didn't intend to fall asleep or to sleep so long," she said. She hadn't realized how bone-weary she'd been since her father's murder. Between the grief and the nightmares, she'd apparently gone without any real, good sleep for too long.

He flashed her a smile, his perfect white teeth visible in the illumination from the dashboard. "Don't apologize. You must have needed the sleep."

"Are you doing okay? Do you want me to drive for a little while?" she offered. "You can tell me the way if you're tired of being behind the wheel."

"No, I'm fine."

"I see the rain is still falling," she said. She sat up straighter in her seat.

"Yeah, although it's lighter than it was. I'm still hoping it stops altogether by the time we get to the cabin."

"At least there's been no thunder or lightning with the rain we've had." She wrapped her arms around herself and tried not to think of her irrational fear of storms.

"I'm definitely ready for some sunshine. Have you ever been fishing?"

"Never," she replied. "I like my fish perfectly cooked on a plate and served with maybe some rice pilaf on the side."

He laughed. "And I'll bet you've never been camping before, either."

"You would win that bet. But please don't tell me there isn't really a cabin and we're going to be living in a tent and catching our own fish to eat," she said.

He laughed again. "I promise you there really is a cabin and I believe you were with me when we bought all the meat at the store to bring with us."

She really liked the sound of his laughter. It was a deep and smooth rumble, and it warmed her insides like a jigger of good whiskey. "So, are you a camper and a fisherman in your spare time?" she asked curiously.

"Not really. I visited the cabin with Glen a couple

of times and we did some fishing, but I'm not really the type to sit around and commune with nature."

"Too high-strung?" she asked, half-teasingly.

He flashed a grin at her. "Probably, and I've been called a lot worse."

"Oh, interesting. So, what else have you been called?" she asked.

"Arrogant, demanding and a control freak, just to name a few."

"People have called you those things to your face?" she asked incredulously.

He laughed again. "Rarely to my face, but I eventually hear about them anyway."

"And are you all those things?" She hoped he said yes. She hoped he was actually an arrogant jerk. That would certainly cool her attraction to him.

"I hope I'm not really those things. Yes, I expect a lot from the people I work with, but I expect the same things of myself. I can be demanding when it comes to hunting down a killer. I never lose sight of the victims and the need to get a murderer behind bars." He shot her a glance. "What about you? What do your students say about you behind your back?"

"Probably that I'm arrogant, demanding and a control freak," she replied with a small laugh.

"Then I think you and I might have issues," he replied lightly. "But I'm sure we'll work together just fine for the duration that we're in the cabin. And speaking of the cabin, it's just up ahead."

She looked out the front window. The headlights shone on a small, rustic-looking cabin tucked inside a stand of tall trees. It looked like a pretty picture postcard, a serene little place in the woods.

Maybe this short getaway would be good for her soul. For the last six months she'd been totally immersed in grief and thoughts of murder. Maybe she could find a little peace here in the charming cabin and then go back to her life with a new perspective. She knew her sisters were right, that she hadn't even begun to move on from her grief. And it was time.

Brad pulled up and parked, and then together they got out of the car. Thank goodness it had stopped raining again. She could immediately hear the sound of the nearby river running in its bank, a sound that, along with the wind rustling through the tops of the trees, was oddly soothing.

"Why don't we go inside and check out everything before we unload," he suggested.

"Sounds like a plan to me," she agreed. They both got out of the car and approached the cabin.

He turned on the flashlight on his phone and stepped to the right of the small porch. He moved aside some of the tall grass and then picked up a rock and grabbed a key that was hidden beneath. He turned and flashed her a grin. "I think this key has been hidden under that rock for the last fifteen years or so."

With the key in hand, he grabbed the handle of the screen door and opened it. It screeched like a cat in heat. "We'll definitely have to find some oil for that," he murmured.

He unlocked and opened the front door. He flipped on a light just inside and then ushered her in. The air smelled nasty, like layers of dust and old wood with a hint of mildew.

The sofa was a horrendous lime-green color and appeared to be lumpy and half-broken-down. A beige-and-green-striped chair looked to be in the same poor condition.

Large cobwebs hung from every corner of the room, looking like creepy, dirty lace. It was obvious that nobody had been inside for a very long time. A large supply of split logs was stacked next to a blackened stone fireplace and the nearby oven and refrigerator looked like they belonged in another century. She was scared to even look in the bedroom and bathroom.

Was this some kind of a joke? Did he really think she would be comfortable here? She wasn't a snob, but this place was absolutely filthy.

She turned to stare at him. He offered her a weak smile. "Maybe everything will look better in the morning," he said.

"I don't think so," she replied. "Are we really going to stay here?"

"We are," he said firmly. "We're completely off

the grid here and my number one priority is keeping you safe. Now, you just relax and I'm going to unload the car."

The moment he left the cabin, she gingerly sat on the edge of the sofa. She might be safe here, but she was pretty sure there wouldn't be any peace. In fact, she'd be lucky if she got out of this experience without completely losing her mind.

Chapter 7

Brad awakened early the next morning, his body aching and burning from sleeping on the lumpy sofa all night long. He got up and quickly pulled on a pair of jeans and then walked over to the window, where no sun shone and instead the skies looked dark and angry. He stretched in an effort to alleviate the kinks in his back, and once he felt a little better, he turned and headed for the kitchen area.

Thankfully there was a coffee maker on the small countertop by the stove. He found the dishwashing liquid they'd brought with them and immediately cleaned the machine. He then started a pot and returned to the sofa to wait for it to brew.

He could definitely use a cup of strong coffee. The cabin was definitely not in the same shape he had remembered it to be. But it had been years since Brad had been here. Glen had said it'd been several years since he'd been here, too, but something hadn't connected in Brad's mind when he'd thought of bringing Simone here.

He hadn't thought of the mustiness, of the cobwebs and the overall neglect of the place. Seeing it through the eyes of a wealthy Colton woman had been particularly disheartening. He was vaguely surprised that Simone hadn't jumped back in the car and demanded he take her someplace else.

It had helped that he had brought along clean sheets and towels. The bedroom had been as depressing as the rest of the place. The queen-size bed had been bare and thankfully stain-free, but cobwebs hung in every corner and the mustiness smelled worse in the small room.

She'd been quiet when he'd helped make up the bed and then she'd gone to bed right after that. The bedroom door was still closed when he poured himself a cup of coffee and sat at the small table for two.

He'd charged his cell phone overnight and he now checked it for messages concerning the case. He was disappointed that there was no breaking news from anyone.

Checking the local weather was equally as disappointing and a tad bit concerning. Rain, rain and more rain. Flood watches were beginning to show up in areas and he could only hope the rain would stop before any flooding could occur.

The cabin was located on a six-mile area on high ground, but it was between two winding rivers that, if the waters rose a lot, would cut them off and isolate them from any outside resources. There was one road in and that was it. Still, they would have to get a ton of rain for the road to flood and cut them off.

He finished his cup of coffee and then, in hopes of putting Simone in a good mood for the morning, he pulled on a T-shirt and grabbed an iron skillet and a pound of bacon. He hoped it was hard for her to be in a bad mood when a man cooked breakfast for her.

He was just taking the crispy fried bacon out of the skillet when the bedroom door opened and she stepped out. She was once again dressed in jeans but had a different blue blouse on than the day before. Her hair was slightly and charmingly mussed and she appeared to still be half-asleep. "Ah, just in time to tell me how you like your eggs," he said brightly.

"Any way is fine," she said and shot directly toward the coffeepot.

"Then I guess this morning I'll make them scrambled." As he grabbed a few eggs out of the fridge, she poured her coffee and then sank down at the table.

He shot her a glance as he poured his egg mixture into the awaiting skillet. She appeared to be staring blankly down into her coffee cup. He decided the next conversation needed to come from her and he just had to wait for it.

Within minutes he had plates on the table for the two of them along with a bowl of scrambled eggs, a platter of strips of bacon and a smaller plate of several pieces of buttered toast.

"Thank you, Brad. This all looks wonderful." She curled her fingers around the coffee cup. "In case you hadn't already noticed, I'm really not much of a morning person."

He smiled at her. "By using my great powers of deduction, I kind of figured that when you stared into your coffee cup like you expected the brew to reach up and shake you awake."

She returned his smile. She looked so pretty with the color of her blouse making her eyes appear even more blue. It was then he realized she wore no makeup and still looked gorgeous. Her skin was clear and beautiful and her eyelashes were long and thick.

"I'm usually not ready to engage with anyone until I've had two cups of coffee."

"Then I feel very privileged. You've only had one cup and yet you're being nice to me."

She laughed. "It's hard to be mad at a man who knows how to do crispy bacon right."

"There's nothing I hate more than limp, under-cooked bacon," he replied.

"That makes two of us," she agreed.

They each filled their plates and began eating. "Unfortunately, it's supposed to rain all day, so I thought we'd just kind of relax today. Maybe it will clear up tomorrow and we can go out and do a little walking."

"I hate that it's going to rain again, but there's no way I intend to just hang out and relax," she replied.

"Then what do you want to do?"

"Are you kidding? Look around us. I'm going to clean. I intend to attack every single one of the horrifying cobwebs in this place just for starters."

He laughed and looked around the room. "That could be an all-day job for us."

"I'm definitely ready to get to work…as soon as I have my second cup of coffee."

He placed two more strips of bacon on his plate and then gazed at her. "Thanks for being a good sport about this place. I had no idea it had fallen into such disrepair. I'm sure when you stepped in here last night you wanted to turn around and run away and I would have been tempted to run with you."

"I'm not going to lie, that thought did cross my mind, but then I realized you have me out here in the middle of nowhere and I wouldn't know where to run to." She got up from the table and poured herself another cup of coffee and then returned to the chair. "Besides, at least the bed mattress is good and we can clean dirty and make the best of things."

"Then you slept well?" he asked and tried not to think about how miserable his night had been on the uncomfortable sofa.

"Despite my long nap in the car, I slept like a baby. What about you?"

"I slept okay." There was no way he'd admit to her that the sofa was an instrument of torture and he'd much rather be sharing the bed with her.

Criminy, even thinking about being next to her under the sheets filled him with a heat that was difficult to ignore. He had to remember that he wasn't here to romance Simone. He was here to protect her from any and all harm.

When they were finished with breakfast, she insisted she'd do the cleanup. While she did that, Brad stepped outside to check things out before the dark clouds unleashed their fury.

The outside air felt heavy with the scent of wet earth and impending rain. The nearby river roared with swollen waters from the rain that had already fallen.

He walked around the cabin, checking windows and making sure there was no way for anyone to easily break in. Even though only a couple of law enforcement officials knew he'd brought Simone here, he was very aware that leaks could happen and there was no guarantee that Rob Garner had no idea where they were.

He was satisfied that the cabin windows were in relatively good shape and he saw no indication of anyone lurking nearby. He knew there were other cabins in the area. From the back of Glen's cabin, he could see another one tucked away in the woods, but he didn't think anyone was staying there.

As he headed back inside, the rain began to fall. He was surprised to see that Simone had changed into a pair of sweatpants and a T-shirt. On the table, she'd gathered cleaning supplies that she'd obviously found somewhere.

"Wow, bleach…furniture polish…glass cleaner and a bag full of cleaning rags, you found the mother lode. But it doesn't look like you found any cobweb cleaner," he said teasingly.

She gestured to a broom leaning again the wall. "That is the ultimate cobweb cleaner."

"Then let's get started."

For the next hour and a half, he attacked the cobwebs that clung in the corners while she cleaned the wooden walls with the lemon furniture cleaner. The rain pitter-pattered at the windows, creating a cozy feeling inside the cabin. As they worked, they talked about their childhoods. She shared some of the funny stories about growing up with her sisters, and he shared a little bit about life with his father. They took a break for a quick lunch of sandwiches and then returned to their cleaning.

Despite the odor of the lemon polish and the faint mustiness of the cabin, the scent of her perfume permeated the air. He wondered if he'd find the source of it behind her ears or down the side of her throat. Or maybe she had dabbed it on between her breasts, where it drifted up and out to torment him.

"I'm going into the bedroom to tackle the cobwebs in there," he said, feeling as if he just needed to get away, to gain a little distance from her for just a few minutes.

"Knock yourself out," she replied.

The minute he stepped into the bedroom, he realized it was a mistake. The scent of her was even stronger in here, and as he stared at the neatly made bed, all he could think of was the two of them beneath the sheets making love to the steady beat of the rain against the window.

He attacked the cobwebs more forcefully than necessary. He jabbed the broom into one of the corners, inwardly cursing himself. He was a professional, not some horny teenager. Yet something about Simone shot his testosterone skyrocketing. He felt like a horny teenager whenever he was around her.

In short order he had all the corners of the ceilings clean. He left the bedroom to find her seated at the kitchen table. "Ah, has the cleaning warrior pooped out?"

"No, actually I think we got everything," she said. "I'm not sure how we're going to clean all the rags I went through. They're all pretty dirty."

"At least the dirt is now on the rags and not on the walls anymore. There's a little general store not far from here with a couple of washers and dryers inside. At least they were there the last time I was here with Glen. We can plan a day to go there and do the laundry," he replied.

"Sounds like a plan." She got up from the table. "And now I need a shower." She grabbed the bottle of bleach. "I'll be back," she said and then disappeared into the bathroom.

He remained at the table and tried not to think when minutes later he heard the sound of the shower water running. If he were to let his mind wander, then he would imagine her naked and that was exactly what he shouldn't think about.

Instead, he got up and headed to the refrigerator. Before he'd cooked breakfast, he'd pulled out of the freezer a couple of nice pork chops for dinner that evening.

After she'd gone to bed the night before, he had unloaded more of the supplies and put them away. He'd left a lot of the canned goods in the car, knowing there wasn't room for everything in the few cabinets.

He knew by her own admission that she didn't cook. So, he knew he'd probably be in charge of cooking the meals, and that was okay with him as long as she wasn't expecting anything gourmet.

Once he had in his mind what he was making for supper, he turned and headed for the coffee table. It had a drawer in it and at one time Glen had kept a deck of cards and a chess set there. Brad hoped they were still there. With no television and with the rain still falling, they needed something to do to pass the time. He breathed a sigh of relief when he discovered the items were still there. Now hopefully she'd be up to passing the time by playing cards and chess.

A half an hour later she walked out of the bathroom clad in a pair of navy jogging pants and a light blue T-shirt. She looked pretty, relaxed and refreshed.

"How was the shower?" he asked.

"Surprisingly good," she replied and sank down on the sofa. "I was expecting a cool drizzle, but it was nice and warm and had a good spray."

"That's good because in just a few minutes I need to take a shower." Although he probably needed to make it a very cold one to douse the fire of desire she stirred in him. "I just wanted to talk to you about dinner. I figured I'd make us pork chops with baked potatoes and a salad."

"That sounds perfect to me," she agreed.

"And I found a deck of cards and a chess set in the coffee table drawer. Do you play chess?"

"I know how to, but it's been years since I've played." She looked toward the window, where the rain was still coming down at a steady pace, and then she gazed back at him. "Do you play?"

"I'm the same. It's been a long time since I played, but hopefully playing will help us pass the time here," he replied.

"Have you checked in with anyone? Has there been any news at all?"

She looked at him hopefully and he knew she was talking about her father's case and not wanting to know about world news. He wished he had something good to tell her, but he didn't.

"Unfortunately, there is none. I hope you know that you can't contact anyone in your family while we're here."

"I figured that out all by myself," she replied. "There's no need for you to tell me what to do or not do when it's obvious."

He looked at her in surprise. Why was she suddenly having attitude with him right now? "I apologize. I didn't mean to come off as condescending. And I think now is a good time for me to go take my shower."

She was silent as he got what he needed from his opened suitcase in the corner of the room and then went into the bathroom. He hoped she wasn't going to be a moody type of woman. The last thing he wanted to do was spend his time trying to figure out what he'd done to offend her. That would definitely make their time together here miserable.

A stab of guilt shot through Simone as she stared at the closed bathroom door. She'd been rude to him, and he hadn't deserved it. But she was so attracted to him she felt like she needed to put a little distance between them.

Watching his muscles work beneath his T-shirt as he'd held the broom overhead and stretched to reach the cobwebs had heated her in a way she hadn't been heated for a long time. Working next to him, she had smelled the faint scent of his cologne and even that had stirred her.

He seemed to be a nice guy, but he could never be *her* guy and being a little bitchy with him was the only way she knew how to deal with her emotions where he was concerned.

This whole setup felt far too intimate and too cozy and domestic and she didn't want her crazy desire for him to make her make a mistake where Brad was concerned. And hooking up with him would be a big mistake. She had a feeling it would be a hot, delicious memory…something she'd never forget, but a mistake nevertheless.

She was ready for love in her life, not an affair with a man who couldn't be available for her in the future. Therefore, Brad was off-limits…not that he'd made any kind of an advance toward her.

Once he got out of the shower and was dressed in jeans and a brown polo shirt, the tension between them was definitely awkward. He went directly to the refrigerator and began to gather the items to cook for dinner.

Neither of them spoke and the silence weighed heavy as it lingered. This wasn't what she wanted, either. This time together was going to be absolutely miserable if the tension lingered for too long.

"I'm sorry I kind of snapped at you," she said, finally breaking the long silence.

He flashed her an easy smile. "That's okay. We're in close quarters and I'm sure there's going to be times when we'll get on each other's nerves."

She moved from the sofa to the kitchen table. She almost wished he would hold a grudge against her, but she was also grateful he hadn't.

She watched as he placed the pork chops in a baking pan and then seasoned them on either side. "You look very relaxed in the kitchen," she observed.

"When I was growing up, I spent a lot of time in the kitchen cooking for my father," he replied. "I took over the job after my mother's death."

"Then you were very young to take on that kind of responsibility." She remembered him telling her that his mother had passed away when he was twelve. At that age she was still playing with fashion dolls and just being a kid.

"Necessity is the mother of invention," he replied. "I cooked all the meals because not only did I need to eat, but I knew my dad needed to eat, too, and he wasn't capable of taking care of me or himself. I cooked and cleaned, and I took over paying the bills, something my mother had done."

"That must have been really tough," she replied.

"I didn't think it was tough at the time when I was doing it. I considered it a way to show my father how much I loved him."

She couldn't imagine being a young boy whose mother had been murdered and who had taken over all the responsibilities of running a household. He must have been a very strong boy to step into the role of parent.

"So, now that you're older, are you looking for a woman to cook and clean for you?" she asked lightly.

He laughed. "I'm not really looking for a woman at all. If one happens to find me and she can deal with my crazy work hours, then she wouldn't even need to cook." He scrubbed down two potatoes, wrapped them in foil and then popped them into the oven.

"I've pretty much given up on marriage at this point in my life," he added. "If it happens…fine, but I'll be okay if it doesn't happen."

"Don't you want children?" she asked.

"Sure, if one day I found that woman, then I wouldn't mind having a couple of kids."

"I want it all," she said. "I'd like to find a wonderful man who respects me as his equal, a man who loves me to distraction. I want the white picket fence and a couple of babies that will play with my sisters' children and keep the family strong. I want what my mother and father had."

She was shocked to feel a sudden rise of emotion as thoughts of her father and mother's marriage filled her head. They had loved each other deeply and it had been obvious to everyone around them.

She swallowed hard against the grief, not wanting it to grip hold of her. "I know my mother envisioned growing old with my father. It stinks that some punk kids stole that away from her."

"It definitely stinks," he agreed. "Whenever there's a murder, there are far more victims than just the person who is killed. It's a ripple effect that affects so many people."

He slid the pork chops into the oven and then leaned against the counter, his gaze appearing a bit reflective. "That's the part of my job that's so difficult, seeing so many people as they grieve."

"I imagine that can be a bit depressing over time." She couldn't imagine having the job that he did, especially speaking to the family members of victims of horrendous crimes.

"It can be, but getting murderers off the streets is what I love doing. I can't imagine doing anything else. By the way, do you know anything about guns?"

She blinked at the sudden change of subject. "It's been a while, but I used to date somebody who enjoyed them and I went to a shooting range with him and shot at targets a few times… Why?"

"I brought an extra gun with me and I'd like you to keep it with you at all times. Could you shoot somebody who was threatening you?"

She frowned thoughtfully. "If I feared for my life, I could absolutely shoot somebody," she replied.

"Good answer," he said with a smile. "So, after we eat, I'll give you the gun so you can familiarize yourself with it."

They continued to talk about his job throughout dinner. He told her about some of the strangest cases he'd worked and they talked about the psychology of some of the most famous serial killers.

The meal was delicious and she found the conversation both fascinating and stimulating. Rain still pattered against the windows, and with the coming of night, a cold chill had filled the air.

"Is it possible to turn on the heat?" she asked after she'd washed the dishes and they had settled in side by side on the sofa.

"There is no heat to turn on, but I can certainly

build a fire to take away the chill," he said. He got up and moved to the stack of wood next to the fireplace. "Thank goodness we have plenty of wood, kindling and old newspapers here."

"I hope there's a lighter there, too, unless you're going to impress me by rubbing two sticks together to make a fire," she said lightly.

He turned and showed her the torch lighter in his hand. "I could rub sticks together and totally impress you, but I think just for tonight I'll use this."

She laughed and then froze as a rumble of thunder shook the cabin. She immediately wrapped her arms around herself and closed her eyes. She was already anxious about the fact that a man wanted to kill her, that she was forced to be in this little cabin with a man she hardly knew. It didn't seem fair that she had to deal with a thunderstorm, too.

When she opened her eyes, she watched as Brad fed slender pieces of kindling to a small flame. Within minutes a real fire began to dance in the fireplace and he rejoined her on the sofa.

"Hmm, that heat feels good," she murmured.

"It does, doesn't it? I've always liked a fire, although I rarely have to build one in June."

Lightning lit up the room and within seconds another loud boom of thunder sounded. "Storms aren't supposed to happen in June," she replied as ridiculous tears filled her eyes.

"Simone, is there anything I can do?" he asked softly.

"Make it stop." She released a small, anxious laugh.

He smiled at her with a gentleness that touched her. "I wish I could make it stop just for you." He scooted over close to her and put his arm around her shoulders. "Does this help?" he murmured.

"It does. I don't know why I'm this way about storms. It's just so silly, but I can't help it." Thunder once again sounded and she snuggled deeper into his side. The warmth of him helped. The very scent of him calmed her just a little bit more than it should.

As the storm raged outside, Brad began to talk about the pets he'd had as a child. There had been a goldfish called Rudy and a frog named Sam. He'd had a hamster named Harry and a dog named Bo.

"One morning I woke up and Rudy was floating belly-up. My mom explained to me that Rudy's soul had gone to Heaven and so we had a little funeral and then flushed him down the toilet."

His voice was so deep and soothing as she listened to him and focused on watching the flames dance in the fireplace. Eventually the thunder and lightning stopped, but still she lingered in his half embrace.

"You do realize I've just been talking nonsense. There really was no hamster named Harry or a dog named Bo. However, there was a goldfish and a frog," he said.

"What happened to the frog?" she asked.

"I'd caught him in our backyard. I kept him in a box for about two weeks and then my mother told me the frog had told her he was very sad living in a box and that I needed to release him back into the wild."

"So Mr. Frog had a happy ending," she murmured softly.

"Definitely," he replied just as softly.

Everything about Brad at the moment was stirring something inside her. The warmth of his breath in her hair, the perfect way she fit against him... everything about him combined and created a storm of desire for him inside her.

She knew she should move away from him. It was dangerous to linger in his warm body heat and in the heady scent of him. She just needed to stand up, call it a day and go straight to bed.

"Brad..." She raised her face and gazed up at him. She wasn't even sure what she intended to say. But his face was intimately close to hers and his eyes held a flame that half stole her breath away.

"Simone," he whispered softly.

She knew if she leaned into him, he would kiss her...and she would kiss him back. And then she would want more...and more from him. Instead of leaning into him, she jumped up from the sofa. "I...

I think it's time for me to head to bed. I'm completely exhausted."

He cleared his throat and stood as well. "The storm seems to have passed, so you should sleep well."

"Then I'll just say thank you and good-night." She went into the bedroom, sank down on the edge of the bed and drew a couple of deep breaths. The storm outside might be over, but a storm inside her continued to rage on.

All day long she had been far too conscious of him. Even when she'd gotten an attitude with him, he hadn't held it against her. He was appealing on so many levels and her desire for him was off the charts.

However, she didn't want just a quick tumble in the sheets with a man she knew was all wrong for her. He wasn't her happily-ever-after and she didn't want her heart to get hurt by her making a foolish mistake.

She had a man who wanted to kill her, but right now she felt the real danger to her was from FBI agent Brad Howard.

Leo cursed at the rain as he rode the motorcycle that Rob Garner had provided for him. Well, in truth it wasn't Rob himself who had made it possible. Rather, it had been one of Rob's cousins who apparently wasn't on the authorities' watch list.

The bike had been waiting for him, all tagged

and legal, and the GPS system Leo had picked up now told him exactly where Simone Colton and her "bodyguard" had gone. It had been so easy to put a tracker on his car when it had been parked in front of Simone's house.

A rifle was fastened to the side of the bike and the saddlebags held not only Leo's clothes, but also a tiny tent and a revolver. Oh, yes, good old Rob had made it easy for Leo.

Rob Garner was rabid about the psychology college professor. He wanted her dead and he had made sure Leo had all the tools he needed to accomplish that goal.

Leo's payoff would be enough money so he could hire a private plane to get him out of the country. What Rob didn't know was Leo would have happily killed her for free.

He was about two hours out from where the FBI agent's car had been stopped for the past night and day. Leo would find a place to hole up, wait for the rain to stop, and then he'd fulfill Rob's wish.

Despite the rain that drenched him and the possibility of eating bugs, Leo threw back his head and laughed with the anticipation of taking another life. Hell, if he was lucky, he'd not only kill her but also the FBI agent who was with her.

Chapter 8

For the next three days it rained continuously. Brad now stood at the window and peered outside. It was going to be another gloomy day, but at least it wasn't raining at the moment. He turned from the window and sat down on the sofa. It was early and Simone wasn't up yet.

Simone. She'd become a sizzle in his blood, a flame that burned hotter and hotter with each minute he spent with her. The night of the thunderstorm, he'd almost kissed her. God, he'd wanted to take her lips with his and kiss her until they were both completely breathless.

He'd thought he'd seen a moment in her eyes where she would have welcomed his kiss, but then she'd jumped up and run to bed. Still, he wanted her more than he'd ever wanted a woman before.

During the last three rainy days, they'd each played games on their phones and then had spent the time playing endless games of chess and cards.

He'd found her a worthy adversary. She was as competitive as him, and both a gracious winner and loser. She was quick-witted and their senses of humor were alike. She challenged him intellectually and he found that totally hot. In fact, he found everything about her totally hot.

In another lifetime he would have vigorously pursued her. But they were stuck in this lifetime, where having a sexual relationship, where having any kind of a relationship other than a professional one, would be all wrong.

His role was to be her protector, and through this ordeal of staying together in such an intimate environment, he hoped they would walk away from this cabin as friends and she would be safe to pursue the life she wanted.

He had given her the spare revolver he'd brought with him and they had gone over everything she needed to know to use it. He felt confident in her ability.

There had still been no breakthroughs on the case. Leo remained on the loose and Jared still wasn't talking. The entire case was basically at a standstill. Brad had no idea how long it would be before he thought it was safe for Simone to go back home, but he knew they couldn't stay holed up here forever.

However, it was far too early in the game to be thinking about heading back to Chicago. He roused himself from the sofa, poured himself a cup of the freshly brewed coffee and then pulled some breakfast sausage links out of the freezer to cook. Breakfast today would be the sausage and pancakes.

He and Simone had fallen into an easy routine. He cooked breakfast and she took care of lunch, usually sandwiches, and then he made dinner. He cleaned up after breakfast, she cleaned up after lunch and then after dinner they took care of washing and drying the dishes together.

Maybe today if it remained dry, they could get out of the cabin for a little while and go for a short walk. Maybe the fresh air would cool his simmer of desire for her, but he seriously doubted it.

By the time the sausage was finished cooking, her bedroom door opened and she stepped out. Clad in a pair of yellow-and-white-striped capris and a yellow blouse, she looked bright and beautiful. But he didn't say a word to her as she beelined to the coffeepot, poured herself a cup and then sat at the table. He had definitely come to respect the time it took for her to fully wake up in the mornings and be ready to socialize.

He placed the bottle of pancake syrup, the butter and a platter of the sausage links in the center of the table and then began to make the pancakes. When he had a stack of five made, he carried them to the table and sat across from her.

"Good morning," she finally said and offered him a small smile.

"Back at you," he replied with a smile of his own. "You look as bright as a ray of sunshine this morning."

"Thank you." She served herself two of the sausage links and two pancakes. "Just so you know, pancakes are my most favorite of breakfast foods." She slathered them with butter and then poured a liberal amount of syrup over them.

"Hmm, I'll have to keep that in mind." He served himself. "Looks like the rain has stopped, so maybe later we could take a walk and get some fresh air."

"That would be great. Maybe if we find a dry enough spot, I could put together a little picnic for lunch," she replied. She licked a drop of shiny syrup off her bottom lip and Brad felt the earth tilt as a fiery heat filled him. Oh, he wanted to be that dollop of syrup that lingered on her lip. He wanted to reach across the table and slowly lick it off.

"Brad?" She looked at him expectantly. She must have asked him something, but damned if he knew what it was.

"I'm sorry?"

"I asked if you thought we could actually find any dry ground out there today," she replied.

"To be honest, I doubt it. The ground has to be really saturated after all the rain that has fallen. I checked the news earlier and there is historic flooding happening all over the place."

Her eyes darkened. "But we're okay here, right?"

"Right. Even though the river is practically outside our front door, the riverbed is so deep we don't have to worry about it flooding," he assured her.

"That's good, but I feel sorry for anyone the flooding affects."

"I just hope the rain is finished for good. It's definitely time for some days of sunshine." At least if it stopped raining, he could spend more time outside, where the air didn't smell like her, where her nearness wasn't torturing him every single minute of every single day.

After breakfast they settled in on the sofa. "Do you want to play a game?" he asked.

"Not really," she replied. "I'm kind of gamed out after the last three days. When do you think we can go outside?"

"I'd say we need to give it a couple more hours of drying out. Maybe after lunch?"

"A picnic sounded good, but maybe I'll plan on tomorrow when things are definitely drier," she said.

A silence rose up between them. She stared

into the fireplace that now held nothing but ashes, and he gazed at her. He wondered if he would ever tire of looking at her, of admiring the length of her lashes and the soft curve of her jaw, the sparkling blue of her eyes and the shape of her generous mouth.

"I'm sorry things are so boring," he finally said to break the silence.

She turned her head and cast him an impish grin. "I haven't found it too boring beating you at almost every game of gin rummy."

He laughed. "That was low. I'll concede that the cards fell in your favor."

"How dare you blame it on card luck when it was my awesome intelligence that won those games."

He looked at her more seriously. "That's important to you, isn't it? For people to know you're smart," he observed.

She immediately frowned thoughtfully. "I'm certainly sorry if I come off as arrogant or some kind of way."

"You don't," he assured her. "I've just noticed you get a bit defensive when it comes to you being a smart woman."

She released a deep sigh. "Maybe you're right. I'm in a male-dominated college world where woman professors are sometimes undermined and overlooked, and in my last relationship my partner often went out of his way to make me feel dumb. So, maybe I've been overcompensating since then."

"That was definitely uncool of him. So, how long were you with him?"

"A little over six months," she replied.

"Why were you with him as long as you were?"

She stared at him as if he'd just asked her what life was like on Mars. "I don't know. I guess I was hoping somehow that he would change but, in the end, that didn't happen and the whole relationship was just a waste of my time and his."

"So, if you could build yourself the perfect man, what would he be like?" He wasn't sure why, but her answer seemed incredibly important to him.

"My perfect man would appreciate my intelligence and not try to demean it. He would want the same things as me…a monogamous marriage and a couple of children. I just want a man who loves me and who wants to build a healthy, happy marriage that lasts a lifetime."

"That doesn't sound like too much to ask," he replied.

"What about you? What is the perfect woman for you?" She looked at him curiously.

"I would want a strong woman who respected my job and that sometimes my hours are crazy. I'd like an intelligent woman who enjoys deep conversations. I, too, would want a monogamous marriage and I'd be open to having children." He wondered if she realized they'd just described each other. "I really hope you find what you're looking for, Simone."

She smiled. "And I hope the same for you. So, tell me about the woman who almost got you to the altar."

"Her name was Patty and I was introduced to her through a mutual friend. She was a barista at a coffee shop and we hit it off right from the very beginning."

"What was she like?" Simone asked.

He frowned. "She was pretty...but kind of loud and brassy. Initially I kind of overlooked those qualities about her because she could also be quite charming and kindhearted."

"How long were you with her?"

"A little over a year. We fought a lot, mostly about my job. She was pressuring me to quit and find another career."

"And yet you asked her to marry you," Simone said with a quizzical gaze.

"I did. I didn't believe she was really serious about me quitting my job and she was pressuring me to put a ring on it. But once we got engaged, our fighting grew worse. She was angry with me all the time. If I missed a dinner or a social night out because of my work, she'd punish me for days."

"Were you in love with her?" Simone asked softly.

He smiled. "I was, but like you with your professor, I kept hoping she would change. I wanted out, but I didn't want to hurt her. Ultimately she broke up with me because I refused to quit my job and we both got on with our separate lives."

"I would never ask a man to quit his job, just like I wouldn't be with a man who asked me to quit mine," she said.

Just looking at Simone right now, any thought of Patty was nothing more than a distant memory. He wanted to pull Simone into his arms and feel her body close to his. He wanted to kiss her over and over again. He wanted to make sweet, hot love to her. Instead, he jumped up off the sofa and went to the window.

"I don't think we're going to see any sunshine today," he said, although the weather was the last thing on his mind.

"Maybe tomorrow," she replied.

He drew in several deep breaths and released them slowly in an effort to get all inappropriate thoughts about Simone out of his head. Even though it didn't completely work, he turned around and rejoined her on the sofa.

Thankfully the conversation was much lighter after that. They talked and laughed about childhood antics and humorous workplace events. He loved laughing with her. There were times it was easy for him to forget that they were here for a reason and not just as a couple enjoying time spent together in a cozy cabin.

But he had to remember why they were here. He'd been in contact with Russ every night concerning the case. Everyone was frustrated by the lack of information concerning Leo's whereabouts. There hadn't even been any sightings of him or clues as to where he might be coming in over the TIPS line.

"So, tell me more about your family," he said. "I've met all of them, but I don't know too much about them."

Her features immediately brightened. "You know January is a social worker. She's passionate about trying to protect the children she's assigned to. She's engaged to Sean Stafford."

"Who is a homicide detective with Chicago PD," Brad added. "He seems like a great guy and he's definitely a good cop."

"I'm just glad they're so happy. Then you know Tatum has the restaurant and now is dating Cruz Medina."

He nodded. "Another good detective. And you're really close with your cousins, right?"

"We grew up with them right next door and it was like they were our siblings. Carly has finally gotten together with the man she was meant to be with, a man she thought was dead."

Brad listened with interest as she told him about

Micha Harrison, a special forces army lieutenant who had nearly lost his life in service to his country. He'd been Carly's fiancé before he'd been hurt and he'd believed it was in Carly's best interest to believe him dead.

"But he couldn't stay away from her. He started following her and watching her and finally she caught him," Simone continued. "And now they're getting their chance at the happiness they both deserve. I think it's all quite romantic."

"And then you have two male cousins. I've had some conversations with Heath and I know he's temporarily running Colton Connections. He seems like a real stand-up kind of guy," Brad said.

"He is, and the best thing he ever did was realize his love for Kylie. She'd worked as his right-hand woman for years and she was there for him as he grieved."

"Jones has definitely been a high-profile guy around the police department," Brad said.

"I know he was warned to stay out of the investigation. I think Jones has a ton of regret. Right after high school, he left Chicago and kind of drifted around for the next ten years. Then he came back and started his microbrewery, which is fairly successful. But when his dad was murdered, I think Jones had a lot of regret about losing those years and not building a better relationship with his dad."

"All I know is him hiring Allie Chandler to go

undercover was the best thing that happened to the investigation. Otherwise we would still be spinning our wheels trying to figure out who the bad guys are."

"I'm happy he hired Allie because they are now in love and hopefully she's helping Jones deal with his grief." She shifted positions on the sofa.

"So, all your sisters and cousins have now found their significant others."

"Yeah, everyone but me. But I'm sure it will happen for me when the time is right." She stood from the sofa.

"Your family is so interesting to me. The fact that your mother and aunt are twins and they married twin brothers is so unusual."

"And then they went on to buy land and build homes right next to each other and had their children at almost the same time," she added. "We all grew up with really strong family ties." She frowned at him. "Do you have any cousins or anyone else in your family that you're close to?"

"No. Both my parents were only children and so there were no aunts or uncles in my life."

She studied him with an expression of sympathy. "I'm sorry you don't have anyone."

"I've never known anything different. Besides, I now have some good friends and coworkers."

"Russ is a good friend?"

He smiled as he thought of his redheaded coworker. Russ had gone with him to several of the meetings he'd had with Simone's family. "Yeah, I consider Russ my very best friend. He and his wife, Janie, invite me to their home a lot and I enjoy spending time with them. They have two kids who call me Uncle Brad."

"Good. Now, I'll bet you're getting hungry. How about some lunch?"

"Sounds good." He got up and moved to the kitchen table while she rummaged in the refrigerator for sandwich fixings.

"You ready to head outside?" he asked her after they had eaten the sandwiches and chips for lunch.

"Thank goodness I decided to throw some tennis shoes into my suitcase. Let me go change into them and then I'm absolutely ready to get out of this cabin for a little while," she said.

She disappeared into the bedroom. He pulled his athletic shoes out of his suitcase and put them on, eager to get outside for a change. He also pulled on his shoulder holster with his gun in the holster.

Minutes later Simone returned clad in a pair of expensive, white shoes. "Oh, those shoes are so going to be ruined," he said.

She laughed. "I know, but when I was packing, I didn't think about having to traipse through mud. I'm willing to sacrifice them to the gods of the muddy earth just to go outside and get some fresh air."

"Then let's go." He opened the door and together they stepped outside. The air was warm and humid, and the wet ground squished beneath his feet.

Brad looked around the area, making sure that nobody was lurking nearby. Even though he was relatively certain nobody knew where they were, he also knew he couldn't ever let his guard down. Simone's very life depended on it.

He saw nobody anywhere around them. He still doubted that the nearest cabin to them was even occupied right now. They first walked through the trees, talking about the wildlife that might live there.

"Maybe this is where Big Foot lives," she said as they continued walking.

"Do you really believe there is a Big Foot?" he asked.

"I'm not sure what I believe, but I do believe that there are things on this earth that we don't know or understand," she replied.

"What about UFOs?"

"I do believe there are things not of this earth that we don't know enough about," she replied. "In other words I'm very open-minded about these kinds of things."

"What about woodland elves? Do you think there are tiny people hiding someplace around here and right now they are watching us?"

She laughed. "Absolutely," she replied. "You

have to say that so if they really exist you don't make them mad," she added in a whisper.

He grinned at her. "You definitely don't want to get woodland elves riled up."

"In case you haven't noticed, I'm really kind of a dorky college professor," she said.

"I must be dorky, too, because I don't think you're dorky at all."

They walked and talked for about a half an hour and then returned to the front of the cabin.

"I want to take a look at the river," she said. Once again, he looked around to make sure they were all alone, then he watched as she walked over toward the edge.

"Don't get too close," he warned. He barely got the words out when he heard an ominous rumble and a tremor in the ground, and suddenly Simone was gone.

She was falling…falling.

It took only a moment for Simone to realize the earth had given way under her feet and then water and mud completely engulfed her. She was in the river. Her brain screamed the words as she flailed her arms and legs beneath the water's surface.

Which way was up? When she tried to open her eyes, all she saw was water so muddy it was impossible to see anything else. Her feet hit what she thought was the bottom and she thrust herself up, finally managing to get her head above the water. She spat and gagged on the mud as she tried to gasp for breath.

Above the rush of the river, she could vaguely hear Brad yelling her name. But she couldn't concentrate on him as her body was buffeted by fallen tree limbs and other debris and she was sucked under once again.

Beneath the surface it was pure darkness and the cold of the water ached in her legs, throughout her entire body. Once again, she fought to find the surface as her lungs burned painfully from a lack of oxygen.

She finally managed to get her head up and she gasped for air as the river carried her. If she didn't do something, she was going to die. With this thought screaming in her head, she began to try to grab at exposed tree roots or limbs…anything that would halt her horrifying progress downriver.

She felt as if she'd been in the water for hours, even though she knew it had just been minutes. She finally managed to grab hold of an exposed tree root, and even though her hands ached with the cold, she grabbed on to it and held tight. Her breaths ached in her chest as she gasped for air.

Mud clung to her face. It was in her hair and half blinded her. She desperately needed to swipe her face with her hand, but she was afraid to take one hand off the root that held her in place. The rushing water buffeted her, and limbs and debris smacked into her.

She should have known that a landslide was possible. She'd been a fool to walk so close to the edge knowing the amount of rain that had fallen.

Now she was going to die because she'd been a stupid fool. Her heart banged so hard she could scarcely breathe. She was freezing, and she knew if she lost her grip on the roots, then she would be swept to her death.

"Simone!"

She looked up to see Brad above her. He was lying on his stomach on the bank above her and he had one hand stretched out toward her. "Grab on to my hand, Simone," he yelled.

She cried, terrified to take one hand off the tree root that held her in place, yet knowing he was the only way she'd be able to climb up the steep bank to safety.

But how could he ever pull her up? She was covered in mud and waterlogged. Was he even strong enough to pull her up? If he couldn't, then she would fall back into the river and somebody would eventually find her body floating somewhere.

"Come on, baby…you can trust me," he cried. "Take my hand, Simone." He reached down even farther so his hand was only half a foot or so away from hers.

If she didn't grab hold of it, she would probably tire and lose her grip on the root. She'd be cast down the river, her body pummeled by the weight of the water and the mud and debris. And she would surely die.

Her arms already trembled with her efforts to hang on and the cold now encased her entire body, making her teeth chatter uncontrollably.

"Come on, honey…let me pull you out. Simone… grab my hand," he cried.

She had to trust that he'd catch her. Drawing a deep breath and releasing it on a sob, she let go of the root and reached for his hand.

He grabbed on to her, wrapping his hand tightly around her wrist. As he pulled her up, she tried to find purchase on the side of the riverbank with her feet to help him. Slowly she rose from the water. His arm trembled with the effort, but his grip remained strong.

When she finally reached the top, she rolled on her back, once again gasping for breath as tears choked her. He got to his feet and then scooped her up in his arms and hurried toward the cabin.

She clung to him, her arms tightly wrapped around his neck and her face buried in his broad chest. Her teeth still chattered with the cold and sobs continued to choke through her. Thank God he'd been able to get her up. Thank God she was now safe.

He carried her directly to the bathroom, where

he put her down on her feet in the shower stall and he turned on the faucets to start the shower. He quickly took off his gun and holster.

He was covered with almost as much mud as she was, and once the water was hot, he pulled her against him beneath the warm spray. They didn't speak.

He held her tight for several long minutes. He then reached up and began to work his fingers through her hair, obviously trying to get out as much of the mud as possible.

She stood perfectly still, sobbing as she allowed him to minister to her like she was a helpless child. He grabbed the bottle of shampoo she'd left on the floor of the shower and squeezed a liberal amount into her hair. His fingers worked to lather and scrub as she continued to cry from the trauma she'd just endured.

She'd been so scared. She'd been so terrified of drowning...of dying. It was a combination of that fear and the gratitude that he'd saved her that kept the tears coming.

Finally, she began to warm up enough that her teeth had stopped chattering and her tears came to an end, although there was still a deep chill inside her. He grabbed a bar of soap and cleaned the mud off himself. He stood beneath the streaming water for another minute or two and then reached out, grabbed a towel and stepped out.

"I'm going to go build us a fire," he said and then pulled his wet T-shirt over his head. Still clad in his wet jeans, he wrapped the towel around his shoulders and left the room.

Once he was gone, she peeled off her clothes and finished washing herself until there wasn't a single shred of mud left on her. Only then did she shut off the water and grab a towel.

She used the towel to dry off her hair and then wrapped it around her and ran from the bathroom to the bedroom. She dressed in a pair of jogging pants and a T-shirt, and then walked back into the living room, where Brad had built up a roaring fire. He'd also changed into clean, dry clothes.

He spread a blanket out on the floor in front of the flames and she sank down, still trying to warm the chill that lingered deep inside her.

He then sank down next to her and grabbed one of her hands in his. "Are you okay?" His gaze searched her features, as if to assure himself that she really was all right.

She nodded, for a moment not trusting herself to speak as the horror of it all washed over her once again. He squeezed her hand. "God, Simone, I've never been so terrified for somebody and it's all my fault that it happened."

"How on earth was this your fault?" she asked as she finally found her voice.

"I should have known the ground was too saturated, that it was possible that a landslide might happen."

He looked absolutely miserable. "Oh, so now you aren't just an FBI agent, you're a geologist as well?" she replied. "It was my fault, Brad. I was the one who got too close to the edge." Her words were suddenly swallowed by an unexpected sob.

Immediately he pulled her into his arms and held her as she began to cry all over again. She buried her face in his chest and his hands stroked up and down her back in an effort to soothe her.

The terror she'd felt played again and again through her head. Once again, she could feel the water and the mud fighting to drown her. She would never forget the feel of her falling…falling into the deepest darkness.

She cried until she thought there were no more tears left inside her. "I…I was so afraid," she finally managed to say. "I was so sure I was going to drown…from the water and from all the mud. Thank God you were there to pull me up."

"You were so brave, Simone. You were so smart to keep your head and grab on to something and hold on. That allowed me to get to you." His breath was soft and warm against her ear. "You're safe now and I swear I'm not going to let anything else happen to you."

"Thank goodness you were strong enough to get me out."

"Failure wasn't an option," he replied.

She knew she should move out of his arms, but she didn't. Finally, the chill inside her was gone and she was wonderfully warm between the heat of the fire and the warmth of his embrace. He smelled like minty soap and clean male.

She wasn't sure when things changed, but suddenly his caresses up and down her back came slower and grew more languid, and she thought his breathing had quickened just a little bit.

Her body responded. Despite the warmth, her nipples grew hard and she breathed faster as a swift, sweet desire rocked through her. She didn't want to fight it. She had been fighting against that desire since they'd arrived at the cabin. Rather than fight it, she wanted to let it loose to run wild.

With her heart pounding, she raised her head to look at him. His face was mere inches from hers, his eyes dark and holding a touch of the same wildness that whipped through her. She parted her lips and he took the hint.

His lips took hers in a kiss that instantly half stole her breath. A new warmth rushed through her and she wound her arms around his neck and pulled him closer toward her.

His tongue touched her lower lip, as if tentatively seeking entry. She opened her mouth wider to allow him in. Her heart raced as their tongues swirled together in a mad dance.

The longer they kissed, the more she wanted of him…from him. She tasted his desire for her and it stirred her on every level. His hands slid beneath the back of her T-shirt, stroking her bare skin and only making her want him more.

A churning, burning need built up inside her. He kissed her harder and she matched his passion with her own. She couldn't remember ever wanting a man as badly as she wanted Brad right now.

When the kiss finally ended, she moved back from him and pulled her T-shirt over her head. She knew she was taking a chance at being rebuffed. But she'd always been the kind of woman who went after what she wanted…and she desperately wanted Brad.

The minute her T-shirt came off, Brad's eyes flamed as bright as the flickering blaze that danced in the fireplace. He yanked his T-shirt off and then reached for her again.

"Simone." He whispered her name in her hair and that only sent her desire for him higher.

His arms wrapped around her back and his fingers went to her bra fastening. "Tell me to stop and I will," he said, his voice husky and half-breathless.

"Don't stop. I want you, Brad."

He unfastened her bra and she shrugged it off her and tossed it to the side of them. She then stretched out on the blanket and pulled him down beside her.

His lips claimed hers once again as his warm hands covered her breasts.

She was on fire with the scent of him, with the way his back muscles tightened as her palms swept across the wide expanse. She felt as if he'd been quietly seducing her for days with his heated glances when he thought she wasn't paying attention, with the inadvertent touches they shared during the course of the day.

His lips left hers and traveled down her jawline, igniting new fiery flames inside her. She gasped as his mouth moved down to one of her breasts, where he began to lick and nibble on first one sensitized nipple and then the other.

She moaned his name with her pleasure. Hunger clawed at her in a way she'd never felt before. She arched up to encourage him to keep licking and teasing her nipples.

After several minutes she pushed him away to take off her jogging pants, leaving her clad only in a pair of wispy pink panties. His gaze never left hers as he stood and took off his jeans. With him clad in just his black boxers, she could tell that he was fully aroused.

He got back down on the floor and pulled her against him, and their mouths once again found each other in a blazing kiss. She was vaguely aware of their frantic breathing. Her heart pounded so loudly in her head she could think of nothing else but him.

She was out of her mind with need. It had been so long…so achingly long since she'd felt a man's desire for her. Still, she didn't want just any man. She only wanted Brad.

One of his hands slid down her belly and lingered at the top of her panties. She arched up, inwardly screaming with the need for him to touch her. And then he did. His fingers slid beneath her panties and danced against her heated flesh.

She clutched at his shoulders as a tension began to build inside her. He moved faster and faster against her, touching her at the perfect spot, and she climbed higher and higher. The tension pulled tighter and then suddenly sprang loose. She cried his name as wave after wave of intense pleasure rippled through her.

When her climax was over, she kicked off her panties and plucked at his boxers, wanting…needing to touch him, to give him as much pleasure as he had just given her.

He took off his boxers and she took him in her hand. His hard length pulsed as she stroked him and their gazes remained locked. "I want you, Brad. I want you inside me," she said.

His eyes flared with fire and he gently pushed her onto her back and then moved between her open thighs. "Tell me to stop, Simone, and I'll stop," he whispered.

"Please, don't stop," she practically hissed.

He entered her slowly and for a long moment they remained locked together yet not moving.

He raised his hands and tenderly framed her face. He kissed her gently and then began to thrust into her. Slow at first, and then with a moan he increased the speed of his hips against hers.

She moaned along with him, her heartbeat pounding as the tension began to build inside her once again. She met each of his thrusts with her own, wanting him to feel as much pleasure as he'd already given her.

Faster and faster he moved against her until she was climaxing once again. He stiffened against her and groaned as he found his release at the same time.

They remained locked together for several minutes as each of them waited for their breathing to return to normal. He then collapsed on the blanket next to her.

He was so handsome with the golden light of the fire playing over his beautiful and perfect naked body. She was boneless and utterly sated. She smiled at him. "That was absolutely wonderful, Brad."

He frowned, grabbed his boxers and jeans and

then got to his feet. "I'm sorry, Simone. That was totally unprofessional of me and it won't happen again." With those words, he stalked into the bathroom.

Chapter 9

Brad stared at his reflection in the small mirror above the bathroom sink. He had just been a perfect example of a major jerk to a woman who had not deserved it. He sluiced cold water over his face and then looked at his reflection again. "You're still a jerk," he muttered to himself.

He'd been so shaken up by what they had shared, by the passion he'd had for her, a passion that had stolen all rational thought from his head.

He had never, ever had such a mind-blowing bout of lovemaking in his entire life. The moment he'd tasted her lips, he'd been lost in her. He'd thrown all caution to the wind and had forgotten all about the reasons why they shouldn't make love.

And what bothered him more than anything was that he knew if given the chance , he would make the same mistake and make love with her all over again.

Now she was in his very blood. He wouldn't be able to look at her without remembering the sweet, hot taste of her lips or how her naked body had felt against his. He now would never be able to forget the throaty little moans she had made and how her eyes had glowed like those of a hungry wild animal as he had stroked into her.

He couldn't regret what they had shared, but they definitely needed to have a conversation about it and he owed her an apology for the way he had just acted toward her. He'd diminished what they had shared and that wasn't fair.

He got dressed and then stepped out of the bathroom.

She sat, fully dressed, on the sofa. She stared into the flames in the fireplace and didn't look at him as he sank down next to her.

"Simone," he said softly.

"What?" She still didn't look at him as she wrapped her arms around herself.

"I'm sorry for being a jerk."

"You were a jerk," she replied.

"I know. I was just afraid if I told you how great our lovemaking was, if I stayed there next to you for another minute, I'd want you all over again."

She finally looked at him, her eyes holding a vulnerability…and a touch of hurt. He hated that. He hated that he had put that hurt in her eyes. "I just wanted to linger for a moment in your arms. I just wanted to bask for a moment in the…you know… the afterglow." A blush colored her cheeks.

"And I should have given that to you, but I was afraid that it would lead to another mistake. Simone, it's obvious we share an intense physical attraction to each other. Acting on that attraction was my mistake. While it was an incredible experience for me, it was still a mistake. There's no future for us and it would be irresponsible for us to think otherwise."

"Brad, I wasn't looking for a future," she replied. "I was just acting on what I wanted in the moment. I wanted you and I knew you wanted me. We are two consenting adults and so we acted on it. It was nothing more than that. I'm well aware of our positions and that when this case is over we will never see each other again."

He somehow wanted to protest her words, but he couldn't. The truth of the matter was that they would probably never see each other again once Leo was under arrest and Rob Garner was no longer a threat.

"And it was a mistake that I didn't use any protection," he added. "Unfortunately, I didn't have any."

She stared back into the dying fire. "If you're

worried about me getting pregnant, I'm on the pill. And if you're worried about catching something from me, I got tested and was clean after my last breakup and I haven't been with anyone since then."

"I haven't been with anyone in years," he said. He hated the topic of the conversation and for some reason thinking about the idea of never making love to her again depressed him more than he wanted to admit. He stared at her profile for a moment. "Simone, I do care about you."

"You have to care for me. It's your job," she replied, her voice emotionless.

"Beyond that, Simone." It suddenly seemed important that she knew she wasn't just a job. "I care about you as a woman, beyond this job."

Once again, she looked at him and this time a smile curved her lips. "It's okay, Brad. Let's just move on from here. Besides, I'm exhausted. It isn't every day that I almost drown in a river." She stood. "I'll just say good-night and I'll see you in the morning."

He wanted to say something to stop her from leaving, but he didn't know what to say, and in any case, he wasn't sure more conversation wouldn't make things worse.

"Good night, Simone." He watched her until she disappeared into the bedroom and the door closed behind her.

He got up from the sofa, too restless to sit still.

The scent of her perfume lingered on his skin, in his head. He walked over to the window and peered out into the darkness of the night.

His mind took him back to that moment when Simone had been standing on the riverbank and then she was suddenly gone. He'd faced down depraved killers before, and had been in life-and-death situations, but nothing…absolutely nothing he'd ever experienced before in his life had prepared him for the sheer terror of knowing Simone was in the river.

Even now, just thinking about it, his heart began to race. He'd watched helplessly as the water had swallowed her up. He thought he'd lost her to the raging river. Horror had gripped him around the throat and then thankfully he'd seen her head bob to the surface.

Thank God she'd grabbed on to that root, and thank God he'd been able to pull her to safety. Standing in the shower with her afterward, all he'd wanted to do was get the dirt and filth off her, warm the chill that had a grip on her and hold her until the fear left her eyes. He'd needed to hold her until the fear for her left him.

He hadn't planned on making love to her. He tried to chalk it up to the fact that they'd just been through a life-and-death experience and had needed a life-affirming action. And of course there was the fact that they had been fighting against their attraction to each other and that attraction had finally exploded. He just hoped they could deal with the aftermath without things getting awkward or weird between them. Still, he knew it couldn't ever happen again.

He turned around, grabbed the blanket he'd been using at night on the sofa, then shucked his jeans and took off his T-shirt. Once he was on the torturous sofa and covered up, he stared into the last dying embers in the fireplace.

He desperately needed Leo to be found and arrested as quickly as possible. Not just to end the case, but to end his time with Simone.

She wasn't just a physical temptation. She was in his head in so many other ways. He loved the sound of her laughter and the way her eyes lit up with her smiles. He loved the serious conversations they had and he even liked the slight edge of defensiveness she displayed when it came to how smart she was.

He loved the little wrinkle that danced across her forehead when she was concentrating on a chess game and her utter loyalty to and love of her family.

The realization struck him like a thunderbolt stabbing through his chest. He was falling in love with Simone Colton. Rather than fill him with happiness, it had heartache written all over it.

Of all the women in the world, why did it have to be a woman he had to protect against a potential killer? And why did it have to be a woman with whom he would never have a future?

If his job and location weren't enough to keep them apart, the fact that she was a Colton, an esteemed college professor, and he was nothing but a civil servant should be enough to squash any relationship he thought he could have with her.

Somehow, someway, he had to gain some emotional distance from her. He prayed the sun continued to shine tomorrow so he could spend a lot of time outside and away from her.

He finally drifted off to sleep with a deep sadness weighing in his heart. He jerked awake suddenly, his heart beating fast and with fight-or-flight adrenaline rushing through him. He grabbed his gun from the coffee table and shot upright.

What had awakened him? What had pulled him from his sleep? He then realized Simone was half screaming in the bedroom. Had somebody managed to get inside? Had somebody broken in through the bedroom window and was now trying to harm her?

He jumped off the sofa and raced to the bedroom. He yanked open the door and then halted. Enough moonlight drifted through the window for him to see there was nobody in the room except Simone, who thrashed and moaned in the throes of what he assumed was a bad nightmare.

He set his gun on top of the chest of drawers and frowned, unsure what to do. Somebody had once told him it wasn't a good idea to awaken a person in the middle of a nightmare, but he couldn't just stand here and watch her suffer.

And it was obvious she was suffering with whatever was going on in her dreams. "Simone," he whispered her name softly and took a step toward her.

She half screamed again, flailed her arms wildly and then brought her hands up to her throat as if fighting off an attacker. "Simone," he said a little louder. Still she didn't awake.

He walked the last three steps to her bed and sank down on the edge of the mattress. "Wake up, Simone. You're having a nightmare." He gently took hold of her shoulder and gave her a little shake.

She gasped and shot straight up. Her eyes flipped open. For a moment she stared at him blankly, as if she had no idea who he was, then with a deep sob she flung her arms around his neck and began to weep.

He hesitated only a moment and then gathered her into his arms. "Shhh," he whispered against her ear. "It's all right, Simone. Was it a nightmare?"

She nodded and continued to cry, deep sobs that convulsed her body. He held her tight and continued to croon soothing things. Finally, her sobs stopped, but she didn't attempt to move out of his arms. "It must have been a bad nightmare. Do you want to talk about it?" he asked softly.

She leaned back from him but didn't completely leave his arms. His heart broke for her as the moonlight played on her slightly swollen and red eyes.

"It's always the same thing," she said, her voice trembling slightly. "I'm in a graveyard and standing in front of my father's headstone. Then his face manifests out of a mist. He begs me to get his killers behind bars. He tells me he can't rest until I do."

Her body began to shake and tears once again filled her eyes. "Then he gets angry and starts yelling at me that he can't rest until I get the killers in jail. His skeletal arms come out of the headstone and his hands wrap around my neck and they start strangling…and then…and then I usually wake up."

She leaned back in, pressing her face against his chest as she began to cry once again. "It…it's so terrifying."

"It's just a dream, Simone. You know your father would never try to strangle you," he said softly. "He'd never want to hurt you. He would only want good things for you."

She cried for a minute and then she regained control. "You must think I'm the biggest baby in the world," she finally said. "I cry over thunderstorms and over bad dreams, and I cry because of my father's murder. I really am a strong woman, Brad. I'm really not a crybaby."

He released a small laugh. "Oh, honey, I know that." He rubbed her back until she leaned away from him. She appeared exhausted but still haunted by her nightmare. "Come on, get back beneath the blanket and I'll tuck you in."

She reached out and grabbed hold of his hand. "Brad, will you stay with me…just for a little while? Just until I fall back to sleep?"

A little alarm went off in his head, telling him it wasn't a good idea, but how could he deny the plea in her eyes, the faint fear that still lingered there?

"Okay, I'll stay here for a little while," he replied. "Just until you fall back to sleep."

"Thank you," she whispered softly. She settled back into the mattress and closed her eyes as he began to rub her back.

There was no way he was going to get beneath the blanket with her. He just didn't trust himself. He continued to rub her back and finally felt her relaxing. Thankfully within minutes she was once again asleep.

He waited a few more minutes and then he got off the bed, grabbed his gun from the top of the dresser and then returned to the uncomfortable sofa to finish out the night.

God, he needed to keep his head about him

where she was concerned. Unfortunately, he could do nothing about how deep his heart had gotten involved.

Simone awakened early. A mere whisper of light lit up the eastern skies. She dressed and quietly left the bedroom and went to the table and sat.

Brad was still asleep on the sofa, and although she'd like a cup of coffee, the last thing she wanted to do was awaken him. She had no idea how long he'd stayed with her the night before after the terrible and familiar nightmare. She was just grateful that he'd been there to soothe her back to sleep.

He was such a good man. He was exactly the kind of man she wanted in her life forever. He was funny and smart and incredibly sexy. He was caring and brave and she was in love with him.

She nearly fell off her chair as the realization hit her hard. When had it happened? When had her physical attraction transformed into something deeper, into something far more meaningful?

Was it when they'd laughed together or had it happened when they were having one of their serious talks? Was it when they had trash-talked each other while playing cards or when she'd thought about the lengths he had gone to in an effort to assure her safety? Had it happened when he'd pulled her from the river and then made sweet, hot love to her?

It didn't really matter when she'd fallen in love with Brad. What mattered was that she was in love with him and there was no future between them. What mattered was that she was headed for a deep and painful heartache where he was concerned and there was nothing she could do about it.

At that moment Brad moaned and he sat up. His hands immediately went to his back and he moaned once again. He stood and walked over to the window. He stretched with his arms overhead and continued to groan.

It was obvious he was having some back pain. The sofa was uncomfortable just sitting on it. She hadn't even considered how terrible it would be to sleep on. And he'd been sleeping on it every night without complaints.

Even thinking about how hard it had been for him, she couldn't help but admire his physique. He was clad only in a pair of black boxers and the muscles in his broad back were well-defined and perfectly toned.

He turned away from the window and jumped at the sight of her. "Jeez, Simone. You scared me half to death. How long have you been sitting there in the dark?"

"Just a few minutes and it's not completely dark," she replied.

"I don't smell the coffee, so I can't believe you're actually talking to me." He reached for his jeans at the foot of the sofa and quickly pulled them on. He then turned on the light overhead.

"I was going to start the coffee, but I didn't want to wake you. But since I was up before you, I'll take care of the coffee this morning." She got up, and as she made the coffee, he sat at the kitchen table.

"Thank you, Brad." She turned around and leaned against the counter as she waited for the coffee to drip through the carafe.

"Thanks for what?" He looked at her curiously.

"For last night, for making me feel safe after my nightmare," she replied. That was exactly what he'd done for her... He'd made her feel safe and protected after the horror of the dream.

"I'm glad I could be there for you. I'm just sorry you have that nightmare at all."

"I'm hoping it will go away forever once Leo is behind bars," she replied.

"I hope so," he said. "I would never wish that kind of nightmare on anyone."

She turned back around and poured two cups of coffee and then carried them to the table. "Brad, I didn't realize how much you've been suffering by sleeping on the sofa every night."

"What are you talking about? It's been fine," he protested.

"No, it hasn't been fine. I heard you moaning and groaning when you first got off it this morning. I know it's hurting your back."

He shrugged his shoulders. "It's okay. I'm dealing with it."

"You shouldn't have to deal with it," she replied. She took a sip of her coffee and eyed him over the rim. She put her cup down. "Starting tonight, you're welcome to share the bed with me."

His golden-green eyes stared into hers. "I'm not sure that's a good idea."

"We're both adults, Brad. Surely we can share a bed and not go where we shouldn't. I know you'd sleep better in the bed and that's what's important." She offered him a teasing smile. "Besides, how can you protect me from a morning threat if you can barely crawl from the sofa?"

He studied her for another long moment. "We'll see how we're both feeling when night comes," he finally replied.

For a few minutes they drank their coffee and enjoyed some casual conversation as the early morning sunlight slowly filled the room. "It's so nice to see the sun," she said.

"Enjoy it while it lasts. When I checked the weather last night, the weatherman said more rain could be moving back in this afternoon."

She shook her head. "I can't remember a time when it rained so hard and for so many days in a row."

"According to what the news is saying, it's a historic year for the amount of rain we've received."

"I'm sure we'll both remember these rainy days and this time here for a very long time to come," she said thoughtfully.

His gaze held hers intently. "I know I will."

"Someday I'll tell my children about the handsome FBI agent who saved me from a raging river."

He released a small laugh. "And I'll tell my buddies about the time I plucked a beautiful mermaid out of the water."

She laughed with him. "Right, a mermaid who was covered in mud and muck and crying her fool head off. I'm sure that's every fisherman's fantasy."

He opened his mouth as if to say something but instead raised his cup and took a drink and then stood. "So, what do you feel like for breakfast this morning?"

"Could you make some more of those pancakes we had before?"

"Pancakes coming right up."

"Can I help?" she asked and was unsurprised when his answer was no.

She watched as he worked, admiring his efficiency, his complete ease in the kitchen. It was far too easy for her to imagine him in her condo, whipping up breakfast for the two of them after a night of lovemaking.

It was a fantasy that caused her heart to squeeze tight with pain because she knew it would never happen. She would never tell him the depths of her love for him. She wouldn't burden him with her love.

He could never be hers, so there was no point. He had his life in DC and she had hers in Chicago. When this ended, he would go his way and she would go hers. Maybe she'd eventually meet a man just like Brad, but right now welcoming another man into her life felt too painful.

She got up to pour herself another cup of coffee as a wave of depression tried to settle over her head. It didn't take long for the pancakes to be ready and they sat down to eat.

Already clouds were moving in and stealing the sunshine that had briefly shone through the windows. The clouds only made her bout of depression harder to fight off.

"You're very quiet," he said when they were halfway through the meal.

She released a deep sigh. "I'm a little tired of the clouds and I'm just wishing this was all over." The latter part wasn't exactly true. She wanted to spend as much time as possible with him, but she also was aware of the fact that spending more time with him would only make it more difficult to tell him goodbye.

"How long do you really think we'll be here?" she asked.

He frowned. "To be honest, I'm not sure. I definitely don't want to take you back if I still think you'll be in danger."

"But, realistically, we can't stay here forever," she replied. "What if Leo is never arrested? Then what? Sooner or later I have to go back to my life."

"I know and realistically I can't give you a definitive answer as to how much longer we'll be here. Right now I'm just taking it day by day and hoping Leo will be caught."

"And you believe when that happens Rob will no longer be a threat to me?"

"I believe once we get Leo in jail, then that will be the final catalyst for Jared to talk and I think he will confess to everything and that'll mean the end of any threats against you." He reached across the table and lightly touched the back of her hand. "Are you sick of me already?" he asked with a touch of humor in his voice.

"Of course not," she replied with a smile. "Come on, I'll dry if you wash." She stood up, grabbed her plate and carried it to the sink.

As they washed the dishes, rain began to pelt against the windows. "So, want to play some cards?" he asked when the last dish had been dried and put away.

"I guess I could take another day of beating the pants off you," she said with a grin even though she was a little sick of playing cards.

They played for the rest of the morning as the

rain continued to beat against the windows. When they decided to break for lunch, she had an idea to break up the monotony.

"Can I help with lunch?" he asked.

"Yes, you can go sit on the sofa and let me take care of it," she replied. Even though it was raining outside, that didn't mean they couldn't have a picnic inside.

For the next half an hour, she boiled eggs and deviled them, then she made a quick macaroni salad and sandwiches and packaged them all in separate storage containers. She then added two of her chocolate bars, some potato chips, and placed it all in one of the grocery bags.

She then went into the bedroom and grabbed the lamp on the nightside table. She took off the shade and carried it into the living room, where she plugged it in and turned it on.

"Now, that really brightens things up in here," he said.

She smiled and then spread a blanket out on the floor. "Consider it artificial sunshine. If we can't have a picnic outside, then we can have one inside." She waved her hands over the blanket. "Welcome to my picnic."

He slid from the sofa to the blanket and sat cross-legged while she grabbed the grocery bag off the table.

She joined him on the blanket and then began

pulling out the food containers. "Wow, how did you know that I love a good picnic with macaroni salad?" he said with a goofy smile.

She laughed and threw a potato chip at him. "You're a dork."

"I thought you were the dork," he replied teasingly. "Besides, on the hundredth day of rain you have to get a little dorky to stay sane."

"So, do you like picnics?" she asked.

"To be honest, I've never been on a real picnic before."

She looked at him in surprise. "For real?"

"For real. If I ever had a picnic with my mother and father, I don't remember it. And after my mother's death, the last thing on my or my father's mind was a picnic in a park."

"Do you have a lot of memories of your mother?" she asked. She saw the splash of grief that crossed his features. "I'm sorry... I shouldn't have asked that," she said quickly.

"No, it's okay. Unfortunately, I don't have a lot. When you're a kid, you just assume your parents are going to be there forever and so you don't gather memories. I have more impressions than any single memories. I do remember she smelled like spring flowers and she loved to laugh."

A warmth leaped into his eyes. "She worked part-time as a waitress, but she was always home when I got in from school. She was soft-spoken and I didn't know until after her death that she was the gears that kept everything running smoothly. Whenever I'd screw up, she'd have a teachable moment with me."

"And what did a teachable moment look like?" Simone asked curiously. The rain that had beat against the windows seemed to have stopped for now. However, the room was semi-dark other than the halo of light the little bedroom lamp provided.

"A calm discussion where we talked about what I did and why I did it." He released a sudden laugh. "And then it looked a lot like extra chores and groundings."

"That's the way it was for me and my sisters. Mom knew exactly what to say to make me feel so guilty and sorry for whatever I'd done." She froze as the sound of a vehicle pulling up sounded from outside.

Brad jumped up from the floor and grabbed his gun off the coffee table. She also got up and stood just behind Brad as he approached the door. He opened the door, his gun pointed in front of him.

Standing on the stoop was a man with a grizzly gray beard and a chubby face. He was clad in a bright yellow rain slicker. "Whoa!" he exclaimed when he saw Brad's gun. His arms shot up in the air. "I'm Nico from Nico's Grocery just down the way."

Brad held the gun pointed at him for another

long minute and then lowered it. "Sorry about that," he said without any other explanation. "What can we do for you, Nico?"

"I'm just driving around and letting everyone in the area know the road coming in has flooded and it doesn't look like it's going down anytime soon. So if you need anything, I'm all you have for now."

"We haven't seen anyone anywhere around here, so I'm not sure who all will be affected by the flooding," Brad replied.

"There's the Ingram family's cabin beyond those trees."

"I didn't think anyone was in that cabin," Brad replied.

"They're there. They're a nice couple with two children. I'm sure they're really sick of this rain."

"Aren't we all," Brad said.

"And believe it or not, there's some people camping here and there. How would you like to be in a small tent through all this?" He laughed. "Shoot me now, right?" His laughter stopped and his eyes widened. "I mean, don't shoot me."

Brad laughed. "Don't worry. I'm not going to shoot you and we appreciate you stopping by to let us know where things stand."

"No problem, and just remember I have some supplies if you need anything. And now I'll just leave you alone."

The two men said goodbye to each other and

then Brad closed and locked the door. He turned and looked at Simone, his eyes dark and troubled.

"So, what exactly does this mean?" she asked, not liking the look in his eyes.

"It means two things. If there's somebody hiding around here who wants to harm you, we can't get out. And if we find ourselves in a tough situation, nobody can get in to help us."

Simone stared at him and her heart beat a little faster. "Surely if anyone is out there wanting to hurt me, they would have already tried something."

"I hope you're right. Right now it's like we're on an island and we only have each other to depend on." He offered her a smile. "We'll be fine."

"Of course we will," she replied, but an unsettling disquiet swept through her. Brad's smile had curved his lips, but it hadn't lightened the darkness in his eyes. He was worried, and that worried her.

Was there really somebody out there watching and just waiting for the perfect opportunity to take her out? Was it possible they were trapped on this "island" with a killer? A cold chill grabbed hold of her knowing they were now cut off from any backup if a killer suddenly showed up.

Leo felt as if he'd been wet for months. He'd been hunkered down in his little tent, trapped by the torrential rain that had fallen, a tent that had collapsed on top of him more times than he could count.

Dammit, he deserved so much better than this. Once this was over, he'd make Rob pay him enough money to not only get out of the country but also enough so he could live the kind of life he deserved no matter where he landed.

He was wet, cold and hungry. And he was majorly ticked off. The only thing that drove him now was the fact that he was going to kill Simone Colton. He couldn't wait to pull the trigger and watch the blossom of blood explode out of her chest. Or maybe he'd take a head shot and watch her brains blow out.

It was just like mag-fed paintball. Load the gun, pull the trigger and watch the paint explode on your target. Only in this case it was load the gun, pull the trigger, and instead of paint, it would be blood exploding from the target.

He'd killed four men before and now he looked forward to killing a man and a woman. The freakin' weather had kept him hunkered down, but now it was just a matter of time before FBI agent Brad Howard and Simone Colton would be dead. His blood sang through his veins as he waited for the perfect opportunity to play a little mag-fed paintball with a real rifle.

Chapter 10

They returned to their indoor picnic, but Brad could tell Simone wasn't feeling it anymore. She was quiet as they finished eating, and when she offered him one of her chocolate bars, he declined.

They cleared the mess and then she settled on the sofa with her chocolate bar and he grabbed his cell phone to text Russ for an update in the case.

Nothing. Still nothing to report. Where the hell was that kid? Where on earth had Leo disappeared to? He tossed his phone on the table and then went to the front window and peered outside.

Was there any kind of danger lurking outside? Or had he overreacted to the whole Rob Garner thing? Had he torn Simone from her home and her family because of his gut instincts…instincts that had been all wrong?

Now even if he wanted to take her back home, he couldn't. Suddenly his head was filled with so many doubts. Had he overestimated Rob's wrath? Was he really just a bully who beat kids and mouthed off to women and wasn't a physical threat at all? Had the carjacking really been a random act?

He glanced over to where Simone had fallen asleep curved into the arm of the sofa. Love for her buoyed up inside him. He had no idea exactly what she thought about him. Granted they shared an off-the-charts mutual physical attraction for each other, but when they'd had sex, love had had nothing to do with it. It had just been raw, wild sex.

Still, he knew he was in love with her. In any case, it didn't matter…it couldn't matter.

It was just a strange twist of fate, or his own paranoia that had them here spending this time together in such close quarters. In reality, even if she told him she loved him, what could he offer her?

A long-distance relationship that would only fail because no matter how hard he tried to maintain it their work schedules would work against them. He'd really never believed much in long-distance relationships. That wasn't what he wanted for himself and it wasn't what he wanted for her.

She deserved a man who was present in all the

hours of her life. She needed a man who cheered her on in her work at the college, one who would hold her through the nights.

It was a lose-lose situation no matter how he looked at it. Somehow, he needed to gain back his professionalism where she was concerned.

Even knowing that, when bedtime rolled around and she insisted he share the bed with her, he didn't put up much of a fight in favor of sleeping on the sofa.

She went into the bathroom, took a shower and then changed into a cotton nightgown with a sleeping moon on the front. He then took a quick shower and pulled on a pair of navy boxers, then went into the bedroom.

She was curled up under the covers on one side of the bed and he placed his gun on the nightstand, then slid beneath the covers on the other side. "Ready for the light to go out?" he asked.

"Ready," she replied.

He reached out and turned off the lamp on the nightstand and the room went dark save for a small sliver of moonlight that danced through the window. The bed felt wonderful after so many nights of the lumpy, uncomfortable sofa. In fact, he felt as if he hadn't gotten a good night's sleep since they'd arrived here.

He lay on his side of the bed, careful not to encroach on hers. It was enough that he could feel her body heat and smell the heady scent of her.

Every muscle in his body remained tensed, waiting for her to go to sleep before he did. The minutes ticked by and he could feel her tension.

She released a deep sigh. "I guess I shouldn't have taken that nap this afternoon."

"Not sleepy?" He raised up on one elbow and gazed down at her. She looked positively beautiful with the silvery moonlight painting her face. He fought against his instant arousal.

"Not very. What about you?"

"I'm tired," he admitted. "This bed feels amazing."

"You should have told me how miserable you were on the sofa after the first night you slept there," she replied.

"I was afraid to mention it. I was afraid you might see it as a ploy to move in here and jump your bones."

She laughed. "I probably would have thought that."

He frowned thoughtfully. "Simone, all day long I've wondered if I was wrong to take you away from your home and family. I've wondered if I overreacted to Rob's threats against you."

She eyed him soberly. "But what if you didn't? I'd rather be safe than sorry." She grinned at him. "I think we're on the same side, Brad. In fact, I think that, no matter what, the time here has been good for me. I've had some peace and quiet and I finally feel like my grief over my father isn't screaming so loud in my head anymore."

"I'm glad, Simone. Let's just hope your nightmares go away soon, too," he murmured.

"Let's hope so," she agreed. "In any case, thank you for keeping my safety first in your mind."

"No problem," he replied.

She closed her eyes and within minutes her breathing slowed and she fell asleep. Brad released a deep, exhausted breath and then closed his eyes. He thought it would be difficult to share the bed with her and not be overwhelmed with desire. However, the lack of any real good sleep for the past week swept over him and within minutes he was asleep.

He awoke the next morning to find that in the night they had spooned together. His arm was thrown around her waist and she was snuggled up against him.

He closed his eyes again and reveled in the feel of her closeness. She was so warm with her shapely bottom curved into him. He was surrounded by the scent of her, a scent that always stirred him to his very soul.

Needing to get away from her for his own good as well as hers, he gently pulled his arm from her and then quietly slid off the bed. He grabbed his jeans and then left the bedroom.

When he was in the living room, he grabbed a clean pair of jeans and a clean navy polo shirt, then went to the coffee machine. He pushed the button to turn it on, but nothing happened. No little green light appeared.

What the heck? He unplugged the machine from the wall and then plugged it in again. Still the power light didn't come on. Great, he thought, did this mean they were going to have to do without coffee? Maybe one of the items Nico carried in his little shop was a new coffee maker.

He glared at the machine in frustration and then grabbed his phone off the charger. Once again, he frowned. The phone was dead. It should have been fully charged.

The electricity. He tried the light switch. Nothing. What in the hell was going on? What had happened to the electricity? Had a storm blown through in the middle of the night? He immediately dismissed that idea. If there had been a storm strong enough to knock out the electricity, surely Simone would have awakened and she would have awakened him.

So, if it hadn't been a storm, then what the hell had happened ? Hopefully this was just some sort of weird glitch and the power would be back on before long. He thought about all the supplies they had in their refrigerator and freezer. Hopefully it would come back on before all of that was at risk.

He walked over to the window and peered out, where the sky appeared cloudless and the sun was rising, promising a clear, bright day ahead.

He returned to the table and sat to wait for Simone to get out of bed. She was not going to be happy with this new situation.

It was about a half an hour later when Simone came out of the bedroom. She was clad in a pair of jeans and a lavender sleeveless blouse that showcased her slender but lovely figure. As usual, she beelined to the coffeepot and then turned and frowned at him. "Are we out of coffee?"

"No, we're out of electricity."

She joined him at the table, her frown still cutting into her forehead. "What happened to it?"

"I don't know. Apparently, it has been off for a while because my cell phone is dead."

"My phone was dead this morning, too. But I thought maybe I didn't get it plugged into the charger good last night."

"I was waiting for you to get up and I figured I'd go outside and see if I can find what the problem is."

"Do you know anything about electricity? I don't want you to tinker with things and wind up somehow frying yourself on a loose wire," she replied with a frown.

He released a small laugh. "Trust me, I have a healthy respect for electricity. I'm not going to do anything stupid. I just want to walk around and see if I can tell what might be the problem."

"Just don't try to be a hero," she said.

He grinned at her. "I want to be a hero, but I don't want to be a foolish hero." He rose from the table. "At least it looks like the sun is going to shine today."

"Well, that's one positive."

"How do you feel about hot dogs for breakfast?" he asked.

"Hot dogs?" She raised one of her perfectly arched brows.

"When I get back in from outside, I'll build a fire in the fireplace and we can roast some hot dogs. At least it will be a hot meal to kick off the day."

She shrugged easily. "Sounds good to me."

"Good, then while I'm outside, I'll look for a couple of good sticks to use," he replied.

She got up and walked with him to the front door. "I'm really hoping the problem is just a fluke and it will right itself before too much more time passes," he said.

"Let's hope so," she replied.

He opened the door and gazed back at her. For a crazy moment he wanted to pull her into his arms and kiss her. He just wanted to lean forward and capture her lush lips with his own.

But any more intimacy between them would only complicate things further. Instead, he headed outside. The early morning air smelled fresh and clean and the sun warmed his shoulders as he began a walk around the cabin.

It was probably going to take several days for the floodwaters to go down. But he needed to figure out if it was safe for her to go home or not. Once the water did go down and they could drive out, he definitely didn't want to make a mistake in his assessment of the situation.

When he reached the back of the cabin, he instantly saw where the electrical wires went into the back of the house. He walked closer to them. He stared at the wires in shocked disbelief as he realized in an instant that they had been cut.

He grabbed his gun from his holster and looked around. Who was out here? Who would want to intentionally cut off their electricity?

He narrowed his gaze and scanned the area. He looked in the trees and in the underbrush, but he saw nobody. He left the cut wires, knowing there was nothing he could do about the situation. He continued around the cabin until he reached the front once again.

He kept his gaze shooting first left and then right in an effort to see somebody and then he noticed the flat tires on the vehicle they had arrived in. Four flat tires. On further inspection he realized they had all been slit. What the hell?

His heart began to beat an accelerated, irregular rhythm. They had no way to drive out of here, and with the electricity not working, their cell phones were useless.

Trouble. It certainly didn't take a rocket scientist for him to know they were in trouble. Somebody was definitely out there. He could smell the danger in the air. It sizzled through his veins.

Once again, he looked around, wondering who was out there. It had to be somebody who had managed to follow them from Chicago to this small cabin, but who? Was it Rob himself? Or was it somebody else…somebody Brad didn't know? How in the hell had this happened?

A boom sounded, sending birds flying from the treetops. A bullet whizzed by his head. He hit the ground. His heart nearly exploded out of his chest.

Oh, yeah. They were definitely in trouble.

Simone heard the gunshot and ran to the front door. Brad was on the ground and crawling toward the cabin. "Stay inside," he yelled. "Simone, get back and stay inside."

She backed up, her heart crashing in her chest as a swift terror shot through her. Oh God, what was happening? Why was Brad crawling toward the door on his hands and knees? Had somebody shot at him?

He got through the door, slammed it shut and then moved to the window to peer outside. "Brad, what's going on?" Her question was a mere whisper as abject fear half closed up the back of her throat.

He pointed his gun toward the window, his entire body visibly tensed. "The electricity wires have been cut, the car has four flat tires and somebody just shot at me."

She stared at his broad back in disbelief. Terror clawed at her insides, a screaming terror she'd never felt before in her life. "D-do you think it's Rob Garner?"

"It's got to be him or maybe somebody he hired, but right now I don't know who in the hell it is. Dammit, if my cell phone worked, I could call and see if anyone in Chicago could get eyes on Garner."

"Does it matter whether it's Rob himself or somebody he hired?" she asked.

"No, it doesn't matter. All that matters is whoever is out there has made sure we can't call anyone for backup, and no matter what the conditions of the roads, we can't drive out of here on four flat tires."

Simone's heart beat so hard in her chest that for several long moments she felt as if she couldn't draw a breath. She sank down on the edge of the sofa, trembling as her mind worked to process everything that had happened.

"I think he's hiding in that stand of trees a couple hundred feet ahead. It was definitely a rifle that shot at me. I might have thought it was some crazy hunter if not for the cut wires and the flat tires," he said.

"So, what do we do now?" Her voice trembled as much as her body did, and her mouth was unaccountably dry. This was all her fault. She had started this cascading waterfall of terror by speaking to Rob and Marilyn Garner that night in True. If only she had walked past them without saying a word.

He turned to flash her a dark glance. "For now we sit tight. I need to figure out if there's more than one of them out there."

More than one? The words screamed through her brain. "How did they even find out we were here?"

"I don't have a clue." He remained at the window looking outside. "There were only a couple of people who knew my plans in the Chicago PD. And Russ knew, but he would never betray my confidence and he needed to know."

"My sisters knew we were going away, but they didn't know exactly where we were going, so they certainly didn't tell anyone," she said.

"At this point it really doesn't matter who leaked the information or how it got out. Right now all that matters is there's a man in those trees with a rifle who took a shot at me."

"So, what can I do to help?"

Once again, he turned and frowned at her. "You could get the gun and go to the bedroom and look outside the window to see if anyone is coming at us from that direction."

She got up from the sofa, and with fingers that trembled, she picked up the spare gun from the coffee table and then went into the bedroom and peered out the window.

Dear God, what had happened to her neat and orderly life? She was an esteemed college professor, for crying out loud, and now she felt like a gunslinger waiting for high noon. She'd laugh if she wasn't so damned afraid.

Minutes ticked by and she kept her gaze focused on the trees in the back. She nearly screamed as she saw sudden movement. She pointed the gun in that direction and then released a gasp of relief as a squirrel ran down the trunk of a tree and raced to another tree.

Was this how her life was going to end? Trapped in an isolated cabin by a gunman? Had she survived the rage of the river only to die now? Surely fate wouldn't be so cruel. But then she hadn't thought fate would be cruel enough to take away her father, still it had.

Tears momentarily blurred her vision. She wasn't ready to die right now. She needed to say goodbye to her family before she left this earth. She wanted to find her perfect love and know the joy of carrying a baby and then giving birth. She wanted her happily-ever-after.

She angrily swiped her tears away. Now wasn't the time to allow her fear to make her weak. Dammit, she was a strong woman and she had to stay strong now, no matter what happened next.

She had no idea how long she stood at the window with the gun in her hand before Brad called to her. "See anyone?"

"Nobody," she yelled back.

"Come on back in here," he said.

She left the window and the bedroom. Brad was still at the front window. "It's been almost thirty minutes since the first bullet flew and I haven't seen anyone move any closer to the cabin. The shooter is still hunkered down in that stand of trees. Unfortunately, he's too far away for my bullets to reach him, but his rifle can reach us."

"Then we're safe as long as we don't go outside," she said, trying to find something positive to hang on to.

"For now," he replied.

She stared at his broad back. "For now? What does that mean?"

He turned around to look at her. She'd never seen his eyes so dark and so focused. That alone made her bone-chilling fear rear up all over again. "I think we'll be okay until darkness falls. My gut instinct tells me that's when he'll move in to try to take us out."

He leaned on the wall next to the window and stared at her. "I'm sorry, Simone. I'm so damned sorry I got you into this mess. I… I thought I was doing the right thing. I really thought you'd be safe here. I don't know how anyone found out we were here, but it's obvious somebody did. Somehow, I bungled this whole thing."

His facial features twisted with what appeared to be a guilt so deep she felt it in her own heart. "Oh, Brad, you didn't bungle anything." Being careful not to walk in front of the window, she approached him.

She stopped when she stood mere inches from him. He appeared positively tortured and she couldn't stand to see him this way.

She reached up and gently placed her hand on his lower jaw, where dark whiskers shot a tactile pleasure through her despite the dire circumstances.

"None of this is your fault, Brad. If Rob went to all the trouble to find us here, he would have already killed me if I'd stayed at home. No matter what happens now, I don't want you to blame yourself for anything because I certainly don't blame you."

His gaze held hers for a long moment and then he grabbed her to him and crashed his mouth down

to hers. His lips were hot…frantic as they plied hers
with a hunger…a need that she answered to.

She wrapped her arms around his neck and
leaned into him and opened her mouth to encourage him to deepen the kiss. Someplace in the back
of her mind she realized this might possibly be her
very last kiss on this earth. And she was so glad it
was with Brad.

Everything seemed so much more intense than
it had the last time they'd kissed. She was acutely
aware of the familiar scent of him, the thrill of
how their bodies fit together so perfectly. Her love
for him trembled on her lips, begging to be spoken aloud, but she didn't allow herself to speak it.
Now was certainly not the place or time to burden
him with the depth of her emotions where he was
concerned.

He finally tore his mouth from hers and then
he placed his hand against her jaw and rubbed his
thumb across her cheek. "It's not over yet," he said.
He released his hold on her and turned back to the
window.

"Do you have a plan?" she asked tentatively.

"I'm working on one," he replied. "I just need
a little more time to get it all straight in my head."

For the first time since he'd crawled through
the front door after the gunshot, a tiny ray of hope
filled her heart…until she saw that his eyes were

even darker than they'd been and his features were taut with tension.

No matter what his plan was, there was always room for error and in this case that error could mean the death of both of them.

Chapter 11

Brad remained at the window for an hour…then two hours. His eyes looked for places of cover and his brain worked to make a plan that would save her…possibly save them both. However, no matter what, he needed to make sure Simone got out of this alive.

Simone sat on the sofa behind him. Even though she didn't speak, as always he was acutely aware of her presence. She was depending on him. Her very life depended on him doing something…anything to take out the shooter.

He'd already failed her. Instead of snuggling into the bed with her last night he should have been out here on the sofa. Maybe then he would have heard the perp approach the car. Maybe then he could have neutralized the threat last night instead of being utterly helpless against it today.

There was no way in hell he just intended to wait for night to come. He'd much rather be on the offensive than on the defensive. He knew there was really only one thing to do.

It was approaching noon now. Within the next hour he'd make his move. His hand tightened on his gun as he contemplated the risk he'd be taking.

He moved away from the window and turned to gaze at Simone. "I need to know one thing from you, Simone," he said.

She gazed intently at him. In the depths of her amazing blue eyes he saw her fear, a fear he knew he couldn't take away and he hated that. "What do you need?" she asked.

"I need to know that you're strong enough to shoot a man, and you need to shoot to kill."

Her face paled. She'd told him when they'd first arrived that she could shoot to save her own life, but the conversation had been theoretical. Now everything had changed and this was for real...very real.

She sat up straighter and threw her shoulders back. Her eyes suddenly blazed with strength. "I can do whatever you need for me to do in this situation. If I need to shoot somebody who is trying to kill you and me, then I will do it."

"Even if something happens to me? You'd still be able to defend yourself?"

She frowned. "Nothing is going to happen to you, Brad. I don't even want to think about something like that happening. Whatever your plan is, it better include you and me walking out of here alive and together."

"That's definitely what I want to have happen," he replied. As he continued to hold her gaze, his love for her swelled in his chest. It tightened and physically ached inside him.

Although he desperately wanted to tell her how he felt about her, it would be the most selfish thing he could ever do. He couldn't burden her with his love when there was no hope for a future between them. He definitely shouldn't burden her with his feelings at this point in time. It would be enough for him if she walked away from him…from this safe and sound. That was the only thing he wanted to happen.

With his love for her still resonating inside him, he turned back to peer out the window. He caught movement in the trees and knew the shooter was still out there waiting and watching.

It was time to make a move. He turned back around to Simone. "The only way to get out of this is for me to go out there and try to take him out."

"No, Brad." She jumped up from the sofa. "It's too dangerous." She walked over to him, wrapped her fingers around his wrist and stared up at him. "Please, Brad, don't do that. He has a rifle and you only have a revolver. He has the upper hand and it's just too dangerous for you to go out there."

"There's enough cover between the cabin and the trees where he is. I can use the cover to get close enough to him where my revolver will be able to reach him." He gently pulled his wrist away from her grip. "It's the only way for us to get out of this. I need to neutralize the threat."

Tears welled up in her eyes. "There's got to be another way."

"There isn't," he replied firmly.

"Then at least let me provide you backup."

"No way. You need to stay inside and stay away from the windows and doors," he replied fervently. "Don't forget that you're the number one target."

"But I could help," she protested.

"I don't want your help, Simone," he said. "I want you to stay here, and if somehow this creep manages to get around me, if he comes for you, I want you to kill him."

He held her gaze for a long moment. "Now, go sit and wait for me. Hopefully I'll be back soon."

He waited until she was again seated on the sofa. He then drew a deep breath and opened the door. He raced to the back of the car and a gunshot boomed. The bullet whizzed by him and pierced the passenger's side door.

Using the car as cover, he crouched low and moved to the front of the driver's side door. From here he surveyed the area just ahead of him. There were a couple of lone trees about halfway between him and the shooter. If he could just reach them, then his revolver would be in play.

Tightening his grip on his gun, drawing several slow, deep breaths to focus him, he finally took off. He ran a zigzag pattern as bullets kicked up the ground all around him.

He reached one of the trees and slammed his back against it, his heartbeat racing so fast he had to catch his breath. This was it. He'd either succeed or fail and the idea of failure was absolutely abhorrent.

He peered around the tree trunk. From this vantage point he could see the person in the woods, but he was still too far away to identify him. He needed to get closer.

He fired his gun and then raced to another tree. When he looked again, he realized the shooter had retreated deeper into the trees. Apparently he now realized Brad was a good shot and the bullets could reach him.

Brad moved again, edging closer to the stand of trees where the perp had been. The rifle boomed once more and the bullet seared through Brad's belly. He gasped in pain and clutched his stomach, where blood immediately began to seep through his shirt.

Dammit. This wasn't supposed to happen. And dammit, he should have taken the time to put on his bulletproof vest. It had been stupid, a rookie mistake, for him to forget it, but it had been locked in the trunk of his car.

The excruciating pain doubled him over. He sucked in a deep breath, trying to get on top of the pain. He couldn't stop now. No matter how much pain he was in, he had to take out the perp for Simone's sake.

He raced to the next tree despite the weakness, the dizziness that threatened him. Blood dripped from his wound to the ground. He felt his heartbeat slowing and he knew he was in trouble, a lot of trouble. Still he raced forward, going from tree to tree as the two men exchanged more gunfire.

He was cold yet sweat beaded on his forehead. His vision blurred to the point he had trouble seeing. The gunshot wound ached with an intensity that half stole his breath away. He took another step forward in an effort to shoot the man who threatened them, but he suddenly realized he was on the ground.

Get up, a voice screamed in his head. *You have to get back on your feet.* He tried to push himself to get up, but he couldn't. His body wasn't responding to his desire.

He managed to roll over on his back and stared up at the blue sky…blue like Simone's eyes.

Simone.

His heart wept with the knowledge that she was all alone now. A darkness edged into his vision. He'd wanted to save Simone, but he couldn't. He could only pray she could save herself. He tried to fight against the darkness, but it consumed him and he knew no more.

Despite Brad's instructions for her to sit tight on the sofa, the minute he disappeared out the door she jumped up and went to the window.

She watched breathlessly as Brad raced from the front of the car to a tree trunk, where he remained for several long moments. Her heart had never beat as fast as it did as she saw him moving from tree to tree.

Then he went out of her sight and several more shots rang out. She waited for him to reappear again. Seconds ticked by... Minutes passed and she had no idea what was happening.

Time continued to pass and there were no more gunshots. Where was Brad? What had happened? What was happening?

She left the window and grabbed the gun on the coffee table. She wasn't willing just to sit this one out. The fact that Brad hadn't walked out of the woods yet scared the hell out of her and spurred her into action.

With the gun clutched tightly in her hand, she

left the cabin and raced to the side of the car. There was no responding gunfire.

From the car she raced to the same tree that he had hidden behind. Again there was no responding gunfire. Had Brad managed to take the killer out? Hope buoyed up in her heart as she raced to another tree. If he'd been successful, then where was he?

That was when she saw it…a splatter of blood on the ground. She stared at the bright red blood dotting the dirt and fallen leaves and her heart stopped.

Had Brad been hurt? Had he been shot? Why was there blood? Why on earth was there so much blood? Oh God, she needed to find him. How badly had he been hurt? She followed the blood trail, her heart now beating so fast she felt as if it might explode right out of her chest.

Where was he? And where was the shooter? The trail of blood took her deeper into the woods. Her gaze shot frantically from side to side. She held the gun in front of her, ready to fire if she needed to.

Dear God, there was so much blood…too much blood, and the sight of it scared the hell out of her. Brad had to be okay. He just had to be. She couldn't face the guilt she'd feel…the grief she would feel if he wasn't all right.

She broke into a small clearing and then she saw him. He was on his back and not moving and Leo Styler stood over him with his rifle to Brad's head.

Everything that happened next seemed to happen in a slow-motion dream.

"Leo." She called his name loud and clear.

He looked up. His rifle began to move upward and she fired her gun. Her hand kicked up from the velocity of the bullet shooting outward. The blast nearly deafened her. She gasped in stunned shock as blood exploded from his chest. She'd done it! He stared at her in surprise as the rifle fell from his hands. Then he tumbled to the ground.

She'd shot him! Not because she'd feared for her own life, but because she'd feared for Brad's. She ran to Leo's side and kicked the rifle away from him, but it was obvious he was badly wounded and unconscious.

She raced to Brad, tears chasing down her cheeks, half choking her as she fell to her knees beside him. Blood covered his shirt and he was unconscious as well. "Brad," she cried. "Brad, please wake up."

He didn't respond. As she stared at the bleeding wound in his stomach, she knew he needed medical help immediately. But how was she going to get it for him? They were cut off from the outside world by the flooding. Her cell phone was dead and he needed help now.

She did the only thing she knew to do. She screamed…and screamed. "Please, somebody help me," she cried. "We need help here."

There had to be somebody around, somebody who would have a working phone and could call for help. Nico from the grocery store had mentioned that there were other people in cabins and camping out. It seemed like she screamed forever when a voice finally sounded from the other side of the trees.

"We heard the gunshots. Is everyone okay?" a male voice asked.

"No, no…we're not okay. We need medical help." She got to her feet. "My cell phone is dead and I need somebody to call the Chicago Police Department and tell them FBI agent Brad Howard has been shot. Somehow, they need to get him to a hospital immediately. Tell them that Leo Styler is here and has been shot as well."

A tall, dark-haired man stepped into sight. He looked at her and then eyed the two men on the ground. "I'm Kyle Ingram, we're staying in a cabin nearby. Are you all right?" he asked.

"I'm fine. Just please make the call for me."

"I'm calling right now," he replied.

She fell back to the ground next to Brad. She grabbed his unresponsive, cold hand. Why was he so cold? "Please, hang on, Brad. Help is coming." Even as she said that, she had no idea how help would get to them. She had no idea how long it would take.

"You have to hang on, Brad." Tears fell from her

eyes and onto his chest. "Please, you have to live, Brad. I…I love you. I…I'm in love with you. You have to survive, do you hear me?"

"I made the call," Kyle said. "Is there anything else I can do?"

"Are you a doctor? Do you have any medical training?" she asked.

"I'm sorry, I don't," he replied.

"Then you can just pray for me…for us," she said, and then tears choked her all over again. Blood continued to ooze from his wound. She'd never felt so helpless in her life.

She glanced over to Leo. He appeared to still be breathing, but it sounded labored. They'd thought it might be Rob Garner in the woods, but it had been the nineteen-year-old creep who had killed her father. And he'd shot Brad.

How had he known they were here? How had he gotten here? As far as she knew, he was a kid without a car, without any transportation or money. The questions flew through her head, a race of questions that, at the moment, had no answers.

Minutes ticked by and her hope of some sort of rescue happening began to wane. Even if law enforcement had been notified, how were they going to get an ambulance into an area where the road was flooded?

Ignoring Kyle, who hovered nearby, she grabbed hold of Brad's hand once again. "Please, Brad.

Open your eyes and look at me," she begged. She leaned over and kissed his cheek. "I love you, Brad. Please wake up."

She continued to sit next to him and talk to him as she waited for something to happen, even though she had no idea what that something might be. She couldn't imagine just sitting here beside him and watching him die, but she feared that was what was happening.

Then she heard it, the whop-whop-whop of an approaching helicopter. Were they here for Brad? Was this finally the rescue she'd been praying for? She jumped to her feet and waved her arms over her head to get their attention.

The helicopter hovered overhead, whipping the leaves on the trees into a loud cacophony of sound. Then a basket with a man inside it dropped out of the aircraft. Joy filled her heart as the basket slowly descended.

She looked back at Brad and the burst of joy dissipated. Was it too late for him? Had he lost too much blood? Were his wounds bad enough that he might succumb to death before he could be taken to a hospital?

The basket reached the ground and a blond-haired man who looked to be about thirty years old jumped out of the basket. "Here, take him first." She yelled to be heard above the noise as she guided the man to Brad.

"You'll have to help me get him into the basket," the man said.

She nodded. With his instructions, together the two of them managed to get Brad into the bottom of the basket. The man rode with Brad as the basket ascended into the bowels of the helicopter.

The man rode down a second time and they loaded Leo. "I'll be back for you," the man yelled, and then once again the basket went up.

As Simone waited, she wrapped her arms around herself, saying prayer after prayer for Brad. Even though she knew they would never be together, even though she knew she was just a job to him, she needed to know he was alive and living his best life.

Her father had already been stolen from her by Jared and Leo. She didn't want to believe that Brad would be stolen from her...from this life as well.

As she waited for the basket to return one final time for her, a thousand thoughts once again whirled around in her head. How had Leo found them here? How had he gotten here? Who was financing the teenage killer?

Still, the number one question in her mind was if Brad was going to survive this ordeal. She grabbed the rifle and then Brad's gun, not wanting to leave them behind for some unsuspecting kid or anyone else to stumble upon.

Within minutes she was being loaded into the helicopter, where Brad and Leo were on pallets on the floor and a doctor was administering fluids. She sat buckled into a seat and watched, praying that Brad would finally open his eyes.

"Where are we going?" she asked the pilot once they were underway.

"Chicago. We have trauma teams standing by at Chicago University Hospital," he replied.

She leaned back and closed her eyes. At least she knew he would get top-notch care at that hospital. While she took comfort from that, it scared her to death that he hadn't regained consciousness. There was only so much a doctor could do in a helicopter in midair.

Before she knew it, they were landing on the pad connected to the hospital. Gurneys awaited them and both of the patients were loaded up and whisked away.

She was directed to the waiting room, where she sank down among a group of patients waiting to be seen. She hoped somebody came out to tell her something about Brad's condition.

It wasn't long before FBI agent Russ Dodd walked into the room. She knew him from the many family briefings he'd attended with Brad. She also knew Brad considered the redhaired agent his best friend.

He immediately spied her and sank down in the chair next to her. "Simone, how are you holding up?" he asked.

"I'm here, I'm okay, but I'm terrified for Brad."

"A doctor is supposed to come out and speak with me as soon as they know his condition," Russ replied. "Can you tell me what happened out there?"

For a brief moment, memories cascaded through her brain. They weren't memories of gunshots and fear, but rather ones of laughter and fun games, of stolen kisses and sweet lovemaking.

But she knew that wasn't what Russ wanted to talk about. It seemed unreal that it had only been that morning that she and Brad had awakened without any electricity. This single day had lasted forever and it wasn't over yet.

She went through all the events that had happened from the time Brad had left the cabin to when she had shot Leo. "I couldn't believe my eyes when I saw him standing over Brad. He was the last person I expected to be there," she said.

"There will be a full investigation into how Leo found you guys and who made it easy for him to get there," Russ said. "And now do you want to hear a little good news?"

"What?" she asked. The only good news she wanted to hear right now was that Brad was going to be all right.

"As soon as I heard Leo was down and in custody, I had a brief interview with Jared. He confessed to everything, the kidnapping and the four murders. With the confession, we can now put them both away."

"That is great news," she replied, and yet her heart squeezed tight. "But it's not worth Brad's life."

He studied her for a long moment. "You care about him."

"More than you know," she replied, her heart aching with the need for Brad to pull through. "Is the doctor even allowed to talk to you about his condition? Aren't there privacy regulations against that?"

"Right now Brad is a victim and I'm a member of law enforcement following up on his case. The doctor will speak with me," Russ assured her.

They settled back to wait. One hour turned into two. Several times Russ got up to make or take a phone call. Simone didn't contact anyone in her family. She wasn't ready to talk to anyone. She felt as if she needed to process everything that had happened before she spoke to anyone. More than anything, she just wanted to know if Brad was dead or alive.

Finally, a doctor stepped out and called Russ's name. She jumped up with Russ and followed behind him as the doctor took them to a small office. The doctor was a small man with a name tag that read Dr. Anthony Montello.

She sat in a chair next to Russ's as if she had a

right to belong there. However, the doctor looked at her, then looked at Russ with a raised eyebrow. "Is it all right for me to speak freely to you in front of her?"

"Absolutely," Russ said without hesitation, and she wanted to lean over and kiss him on the cheek in gratitude.

"So, the bullet that your agent received struck around his appendix area and exited his back. Unfortunately, the appendix ruptured. Thank goodness he was brought in when he was. We performed an emergency appendectomy and cleaned up a few other areas and we're hitting him with plenty of antibiotics. The surgery went well and he's now out of danger and resting peacefully in a room."

Simone gasped in relief. Thank goodness the helicopter had come when it had. Brad was going to be okay and that was all that mattered. "Can I see him?" she asked.

"He's still asleep from the anesthesia, but he's in room 1045. If he does wake up, I don't want him stressed. His body has been through a lot."

"I promise I won't stress him," she replied.

"As far as the other patient who was brought in with Agent Howard, I spoke briefly to the other surgeon that attended to him before I came out here to speak to you," the doctor said. "He's been touch and go and they are performing surgery on him as we speak. The bullet ripped through his stomach wall and bounced around in there doing some damage before exiting out his back. I'll have more information for you once the surgery is finished."

"Thank you, Dr. Montello." Russ stood as did the doctor. The two men shook hands, Simone got out of her chair and a moment later she and Russ were in a hospital hallway.

"Well, I guess I know where you're headed," Russ said to her.

"I just need to see him. I…I need to assure myself that he's really okay. He almost died protecting me, Russ. He was a real hero out there."

Russ smiled at her. "He was just doing his job, Simone. Could you please call me when you're ready to leave the hospital? I want to provide you an armed escort to take you home."

She looked at him in surprise. "Why? Leo isn't exactly going to jump off the operating table to come after me."

"He won't, but we can't lose track of the fact that Brad was worried about Rob Garner coming after you," Russ replied. "What I suggest is we get you home safely and then you stay put for the next several days until the investigation has a little more information for all of us."

She eyed him soberly. "I'll call you when I'm ready to leave." It would be an insult to Brad if after all he'd gone through she didn't take Russ's assessment and advice seriously.

He nodded and the two said their goodbyes. She wasn't sure where he was headed off to, but she was headed straight to Brad's room.

He was just doing his job. Russ's words played and replayed in her head as she rode the elevator up to the tenth floor. Of course that was what Brad had been doing. Just because the two of them succumbed to their sexual yearnings didn't mean he loved her. It was just something that had happened while he was doing his job.

When she reached the doorway of room 1045, she stood in the threshold and her heart constricted tight in her chest. Brad was in the bed, an IV attached to his arm and his face as pale as the pillowcase behind him. The room was in semidarkness and his eyes were closed.

Quietly she made her way to the chair next to his bed and sank down. She just wanted to gaze at him, to memorize his features and keep them forever in her brain...in the very depths of her heart.

As she sat there, all their time together rushed through her brain, from the moment she had first met him to this moment in time.

He was the man of her dreams, the man she wished she could spend the rest of her life with. And it broke her heart because she knew that wasn't going to happen. Still, it was going to be difficult for any other man to find a place in her heart for a very long time to come.

She must have been exhausted by the day's events for she fell into a deep sleep in the chair. When she finally awoke, it was to faint morning light spilling through the hospital window.

She looked at Brad and was shocked to discover him gazing at her. "Brad," she said softly. She got up out of the chair and moved to stand at his bedside.

"Simone," he replied, his voice sounding slightly hoarse and dry.

There was a cup of water with a straw on a metal table and she picked it up and offered him a drink. He drew on the straw for a moment and then she placed the cup back on the tray.

"When I got to the hospital last night, I regained consciousness long enough to learn what occurred after I passed out. I know now what happened to me and I was told about what you did," he said.

His brows knit together and he frowned at her. "Dammit, Simone, you could have been killed." His voice had a ring of anger. "You should have never come out to find me."

She stared at him in stunned surprise. "If I hadn't, then you would be dead and Leo wouldn't be in this hospital under police custody right now. I did what I had to do." She held his gaze with a touch of anger of her own.

He finally looked away and drew in a deep breath. "I'm sorry," he said and gazed at her once again. "I didn't mean to jump at you. I'm glad things have turned out the way they have. A full investigation is going on and I need to know you'll still be safe from Rob Garner."

"I'm supposed to call Russ when I'm ready to leave here and he's providing an officer to take me home."

"Good. I need to know you're still staying safe until the investigation is over and we know all the pieces. In the meantime, I imagine I'll be in here for a couple of days and then I'll be heading back to DC."

Oh, the words broke her heart even though she had known this was what was going to happen. "Would you stop by my place to tell me goodbye before you leave town?"

"Absolutely, and I'll make sure Russ keeps you informed about the ongoing investigation." His voice was completely professional and sounded weary and she knew he'd distanced himself from her.

She forced a smile to her lips. "Thank you, Brad, for everything."

"No need to thank me. I was just doing my job," he replied.

Just doing his job. She'd grown to hate those words. At that moment a nurse entered the room. Simone murmured a goodbye and then stepped out. She held it together when she called Russ and then waited for an officer to arrive. She kept her emotions in check as the officer drove her home.

When she finally stepped into her condo and was all alone, she collapsed on her sofa and began to cry. She cried for the wounds Brad had suffered in trying to protect her. Her heart wept with the love she had for him. Her feelings for him had been so unexpected, so achingly real, and now she had no idea where to put those emotions.

Somehow, someway, she had to get over him. But right now with everything, with him so fresh in her mind, she felt like she'd never be able to put her love for him behind her and move on.

Chapter 12

"Hey, man," Brad greeted Russ as he came into the hospital room. He'd been in the hospital for five long days and he was going stir-crazy. He'd been spending most of his time sleeping. The antibiotics were doing their job and he'd been weaned off his pain meds.

"How you feeling?" Russ asked as he sank into the chair next to Brad's hospital bed.

"Physically I'm feeling pretty good. Mentally I'm going nuts. I need to get out of here and get back to work."

"You need to follow your doctor's orders and stay put as long as he thinks you need to," Russ replied. "But the good news is I've come with updates from the investigation."

"Good. Tell me all," Brad said eagerly. He needed something, anything to think about other than Simone.

"Rob Garner has been arrested," Russ said.

Brad looked at him in surprise. "For what?"

"He's being charged with conspiracy to commit murder, aiding and abetting, and a number of other crimes."

"So he was helping Leo." Brad raised the head of his bed a couple of inches.

"Leo told us everything. It was Rob, through a cousin of his, who got Leo the motorcycle that he drove to follow you to the cabin. The cousin swears that he had no idea what Rob was up to. Anyway, Leo managed to put a tracker on your car before you left Chicago."

"Damn, I should have checked for something like that before we headed to the cabin. But it never entered my mind." Inwardly he cursed himself. It had been his mistake that had brought Leo to them. He was an FBI agent and a nineteen-year-old kid had gotten one over on him.

"According to Leo, Rob was crazed with the need to kill you and Simone," Russ continued. "So, Leo rode the motorcycle to the woods near the cabin, where he camped out in a tent during the rain and waited for an opportunity to take you both out."

"What did he hope to gain?" Brad asked.

"Rob really believed that if the two of you were killed, then it would complicate things and slow down the case against Jared. It would give them more time to build a defense case."

Brad shook his head. "I was pretty sure that was the motive, but if we'd both died, that wouldn't have slowed the case against Jared and Leo at all."

"All I can tell you is that's what Leo said Rob believed."

"I swear, the longer I'm in this business, the crazier I think people are," Brad replied.

For the next twenty minutes or so, the two men continued to talk about the case. Leo was recovering from his surgery but was still listed on the critical list. Brad hoped the kid lived so he could spend the rest of his life in prison for the four men he'd killed and for almost killing Brad and Simone. Death at this point was far too easy for the psychopath.

"Have you spoken with Simone?" Brad finally asked the question that he'd wanted to ask since the moment Russ had appeared. When Brad hadn't been sleeping, thoughts of her had consumed him.

"Yeah, I called her to let her know that Rob had been arrested and she was no longer in any danger."

"I'm sure that made her happy." Instantly Brad's

mind pulled up a vision of Simone laughing and her beautiful eyes sparkling.

"I don't know about it making her happy, but I'm sure she was relieved to hear the news," Russ replied. Russ looked at him for a long moment. "You're really into her, aren't you?"

"I'm crazy about her." Brad's love for Simone pressed against his chest, momentarily making it difficult for him to draw a breath.

"So, what are you going to do about it?" Russ asked.

Brad released another heavy sigh. "Nothing. I'm going to go back to DC and put this all behind me."

"She seems pretty crazy about you, too."

Brad's heart hurt just a little bit more. "I'll admit that we got really close in that cabin, but I'm sure now that she's had a few days to process everything, she's back to reality. I'm sure she now realizes that any feelings she might have had for me were due to our circumstances and nothing more."

"Whatever, dude," Russ replied. "I've just never seen the look on your face that I've seen when you just speak her name." He gazed at Brad for another long moment and then stood. "In any case, it's time for me to get back to work. I'll stop in tomorrow."

"Thanks, Russ." He watched as his colleague and friend left the room.

Brad lowered the head of his bed. He closed his eyes as his thoughts were consumed with Simone.

Under different circumstances she would have been the woman he wanted to marry, the woman he'd want to have his children.

He knew she'd make an awesome wife and an incredible mother. She was the woman who would fill all his needs and all his wants and it completely broke his heart that it wasn't going to happen with her.

Whatever they'd shared in that cabin had been fantasy. Now that she was back in her condo, back with her family and friends, he was sure she'd already moved on from their experience.

He would just have to figure out a way to return to his life and forget about her. But right now that seemed impossible.

It was five days later that he was finally released and Russ picked him up from the hospital to take him to his hotel room.

"We're done here," Russ said. "Chicago PD is now in charge of the case and we have airline tickets waiting for us to head back home tomorrow. I have keys to a vehicle you can use today and then tomorrow we have a car picking us up at ten to take us to the airport."

"Sounds good," Brad said, but he was already thinking about his promise to tell Simone goodbye before he left.

Once they were back at the hotel, Brad took a long shower and changed into a pair of clean jeans and a green polo shirt. Although he was healing up nicely, he hadn't quite regained all his energy, but the doctor had assured him he'd return to normal with a little more time.

The one thing he wanted to do right now was head over to Simone's condo to tell her goodbye. It was going to be one of the most difficult moments in his life, but he needed to get it done. He needed to get it over with as soon as possible.

As he drove, he steeled himself for seeing her again. He tried to shut off all his emotions. He knew it was going to hurt to tell her goodbye. He knew it was going to hurt badly, but it was time for him to move on. His work here in Chicago was done, and that meant it was time for him to move on and prepare for his next case.

He pulled up and parked in front of her condo. He didn't even know if she was home or not. He hadn't called beforehand. He got out of his car and drew in several deep breaths and released them slowly.

When he felt centered enough, when he felt strong enough, he walked to her front door and knocked. His heart fluttered as he heard somebody approaching the door from the other side.

Then it opened and she stood before him. In an instant he took in the sight of her. She was clad in jeans and a bright pink T-shirt that emphasized the blue of her eyes. They were eyes that widened at the sight of him.

"Brad," she said softly, and one of her hands reached up to smooth her hair. "Please…come in." She opened the door wider to allow him entry.

He stepped inside and instantly her scent surrounded him, that evocative, wonderful scent that would always remind him of her. She gestured him toward the sofa. He sank down on one end and she sat right next to him. "How are you doing?" she asked as her gaze searched his features.

"I'm doing well. I just got out of the hospital a little while ago and I leave to head back to DC tomorrow," he replied.

"Oh." She looked surprised. "So soon? What about the case?"

"It's pretty well wound up with the boys both confessing to the murders. Chicago PD and the prosecutor will take things from here. I hope you and your family have found some closure knowing those two young men will go to prison for a very long time." He looked at some point just over her head because it was just too painful to gaze directly at her.

"There will never be complete closure. There will always be a hole where my father once was, but I think we're all coming to a kind of peace now," she replied.

He finally met her gaze with his. "I'm glad, Simone. That's all I've really wanted for you since the beginning of this case."

The depth of her blue eyes filled with emotion, although he couldn't discern exactly what emotion it was. "Brad," she said softly. "I don't want you to go, but before you do, I just want you to know that I'm in love with you."

The unexpected words hung in the air between them. He stared at her in stunned surprise. This was the last thing he'd expected from her. And as much as the words torched through his heart, he didn't really believe them.

"Simone, we went through a very intense time together. It was a crazy time with some life-and-death situations. It's only natural that you might think you have some feelings for me because of everything we went through together," he said. "Once you get some time and distance from everything, you'll realize you don't really love me, that what you feel is probably gratitude."

She frowned at him. "Brad, I know what my feelings are for you. It wasn't in the life-and-death situations that I fell in love with you. It was in the quiet moments we shared. I fell in love with you when we had our long talks and when we laughed together." Tears filled her eyes. "Please don't try to minimize my love for you."

"Simone," he replied softly…painfully. "We both have lives to get back to. We're from totally different worlds. You have your life here and I have mine in DC." He got up from the sofa. He couldn't sit next to her another moment. He wanted her so badly, but he didn't see a life together for them beyond this moment in time. "Simone, I've got to go." He took several steps toward the front door.

She got up from the sofa and followed him. Before he could open the door, she stopped him by placing her hand on his arm. "Brad, I know you have to go. I know you don't believe that I love you with all my heart and soul, but could you please kiss me one last time before you leave?"

Her eyes were filled with such yearning it nearly stole his breath away. Even though he knew it was all wrong, he wanted to kiss her. He wanted one last taste of her to take with him.

Before he realized what he was doing, he gathered her into his arms. She leaned into him and raised her face. He took her mouth with his, and with all the love and all the passion that was in his heart, he kissed her.

She opened her mouth to him and he deepened the kiss, swirling his tongue with hers and building a sharp desire inside him. She wrapped her arms around his neck and pulled him even more intimately close to her.

He wanted to pick her up in his arms and carry her into her bedroom. He wanted to crawl into her bed and make love with her. But someplace in the back of his mind was a voice of reason that told him that would be a huge mistake. It was time to say goodbye for the last time.

He finally pulled away from her and took a step back. A wealth of emotions tightened his chest as he gazed at her. "It's time for me to say goodbye, Simone. I care about you more than you'll ever know, but I do think this is gratitude."

He didn't wait for her response. If he stayed another minute and looked at her, he would crumble and tell her just how much he loved her, and that would only complicate things for both of them moving forward.

He walked back to his car and got inside. He dropped his head back and closed his eyes. His heart ached like it never had before. No woman had ever gotten so deeply into his heart like Simone had. He couldn't imagine loving another woman like he loved her.

He finally put the car into gear and drove away. He wondered how long it would take for him to feel whole again. How long would it take for him to forget how much he loved Simone Colton?

Forever, his heart whispered. It would take him forever to get over this heartache.

It had been just a little over a week since Brad had left town and still Simone found herself bursting into tears at unexpected moments during the days and nights. She tried to fight against the depression that challenged her. She kicked herself for losing it so much over a man.

But he hadn't just been any man. He'd been *her* man…the one she'd wanted to build a life with. He'd been the man she'd been waiting her whole life for. She'd somehow believed that when she'd confessed her love for him that he would have taken her in his arms and professed his love for her and they would have figured out some kind of a happily-ever-after. But that hadn't happened.

He'd easily walked away from her when she'd believed he truly cared for her. Had she been wrong when she'd thought she'd seen love shining from his eyes? Had she mistaken the caring in his eyes when he thought she wasn't looking?

It didn't matter today. It was the Fourth of July and within minutes she was going to head to her family home for a big barbecue with the whole family.

It was a day for celebration…for freedom and the love of family and country. After the barbecue there would be a display of fireworks to finish out the night.

She dressed in a pair of white jeans and a red, white and blue blouse and at four o'clock she left her condo to head to her mother's home.

As she drove, she anticipated spending time not only with her sisters, but also with her cousins. It was time they all had some fun together. They were all beginning to heal from the deep wounds the murders had created. After almost seven months, it was time to heal.

It was amazing to her that once she found out Jared had confessed and Leo was in custody, her nightmares had stopped. Finally, she felt as if her father had gotten the justice he deserved, the justice he'd needed to move on. And she truly believed he was now resting in peace.

By the time she arrived at the house, things were already in full swing. Three picnic tables covered in red tablecloths had been set up in the common area between the two homes. On top of each picnic table were red, white and blue floral arrangements.

The air was redolent with the scent of baked beans and potato salad, of deviled eggs and a warm barbecue grill awaiting burgers and other meats.

January and her fiancé, Sean Stafford, were playing cornhole against Micha and Carly. All of them were laughing as trash talk went back and forth and Jones and Allie provided comic relief from the sidelines.

Tatum and Cruz stood at the barbecue grill next to Heath and Kylie, the two men arguing about the best barbecue sauce for ribs.

Meanwhile Simone's mother and her aunt sat side by side in lawn chairs. Simone walked over and kissed her mother on the cheek and then kissed her aunt Fallon on her forehead.

"Sit down, honey," her mother said and gestured to the lawn chair that was still vacant next to her.

It wasn't lost on Simone that out of her sisters and her cousins and of course, aside from her mother and aunt, she was the only one here without a significant other. Her heart ached with the absence of Brad, as it had since the moment he'd walked out of her door.

"Did you make your famous potato salad?" she asked her mother.

"I did, and your aunt Fallon made the baked beans," Simone's mother replied.

"And Tatum bought several other side dishes from True," her aunt Fallon said. "Along with dessert."

Simone continued to visit with the two older women, grateful to see that a lot of the sorrow that had clung to them had eased away. While she knew the twin sisters would never get over the loss of their husbands, Simone was just grateful to see them moving on.

She left her chair only when Heath asked her to be his partner in the cornhole game. After several games, she sat at one of the picnic tables as the men began to cook the meats.

As dinner commenced, there was a lot of laughter. When the meal was almost finished, somebody suggested that they go around the table and tell what they were thankful for.

"Aunt Fallon, you start," Simone said, and they all fell silent and looked at Fallon expectantly.

"I'm happy to announce that I'm looking forward to getting back to our interior design business and Farrah and I are planning a trip to Europe together."

All the children clapped and hooted at the news. Simone smiled at her mother proudly. She was so happy that the two sisters could finally breathe again after the tragedy and a trip to Europe was a great way to help the two sisters leave the bad times behind and kick-start their design business.

"I'll go next," Heath said and stood from his seat. "First of all, I want to thank you all for your support in allowing me to be the new, permanent president of Colton Connections. And today I filed for the first patent of my own."

Once again, cheers rang out. "Apparently, the apple didn't fall far from the genetic tree," Simone said, thinking of her father and uncle's genius when it came to patents that were often bought for huge chunks of cash, or sent off for developmental application.

"Me next, me next," January exclaimed and jumped to her feet. She pulled Sean to stand next to her. "I just want to let you all know that our wedding is going to be moving up…because we're expecting…twins!"

Simone and Tatum got up and hugged their sister with excitement. "And so the next generation begins," Farrah said as she dabbed at happy tears with her napkin.

"Next," January said, and she and Sean sat back down.

Jones stood and cleared his throat. "I've named a new manager at the microbrewery. As much as I love you all, I've decided to do some traveling with this woman." He grabbed Allie's hand and kissed the back of it. "While she's investigating stories around the country, I'll be sharing in the adventures with her."

It was great to see Jones happy. He'd taken the death of his father very hard, but Simone had a feeling he and Allie had a wonderful future together.

Then it was Carly's turn to tell everyone that she and Micha had decided to sell her little bungalow and purchase a home closer to everyone so they could start on building a family.

Tatum then jumped up from her chair, her eyes sparkling brightly. "Yesterday I signed a fairly lucrative contract with a publisher for my cookbook. And that's not the only thing that happened yesterday." She held up her left hand, and on the ring finger was a beautiful diamond ring. "I got a cookbook deal and a fiancé," she said joyfully.

Once again, congratulations rang in the air and then everyone turned and looked at Simone expectantly. She smiled and stood, and then to her horror, she promptly burst into tears.

Much to her embarrassment everyone rallied around her while she insisted she was fine. She tried to convince everyone they were just happy tears because she was so thrilled that everyone had found their special person and had great plans for their futures.

The porch lights came on against the fall of dusk as they all settled back in for dessert. Farrah and Fallon went inside and came out a few minutes later with strawberry shortcake from True and the housekeeper followed behind them with a huge red, white and blue cake complete with lit baby sparklers.

They were in the middle of dessert when the housekeeper returned and bent down next to Simone. "There's somebody here to see you, Miss Simone. He's waiting in the foyer."

Simone excused herself and left the table. Who would be here to see her? Was it possible Wayne, the history professor, was coming to see her in an effort to convince her to go round two with him? He'd called her several times since he'd learned about her ordeal at the cabin. But she definitely had no interest in going there again.

Or was it possible…? She was afraid to hope. She was afraid to even wish in case she was bitterly disappointed. She stepped into the foyer and saw him. He was turned away from her and star-

ing out the window, but she would have recognized
that broad back anywhere.

Brad. His name fluttered in her head…in her
heart. What was he doing here? Did he have something new to discuss with her concerning the case?
Something that couldn't be settled by a phone call?

"Brad," she half whispered his name.

He whirled around at the sound of her voice.
"Simone."

"What are you doing here? Has something come
up with the case?" she asked. The very sight of him
caused her love for him to slam into her all over
again. She crossed her arms in front of her as if that
would defend her against her own emotions where
he was concerned.

"No, I'm not here about the case," he said. His
eyes were dark and unfathomable. "Simone, I'm
sorry to interrupt what I'm sure is a family gather-
ing, but it's important that I speak with you."

"About what?" Her heart began to beat an irregular rhythm in her chest.

"To start with, I want to talk about me."

She frowned. "Okay…what about you?" This
whole thing seemed odd and surreal. He came here
to talk about himself?

He gazed at some point over her head. "I was
sure when I left here that I was doing the right
thing. I was sure that the best thing I could do for

you was to walk away and let you get on with your life. In my head it was the noble thing to do."

He released a small, humorless laugh. "I realized quickly that being noble wasn't going to work for me. Even though I threw myself back into my work, I couldn't get you out of my head."

His gaze finally met hers. They were a beautiful golden green today, and she wanted nothing more than to fall into their depths, but still she was afraid.

"Simone, all I can think about is you. I miss laughing with you. I miss talking to you. I know I'm taking a chance on coming here. I'm taking the chance that your mind hasn't changed about me. And even if it has, I have to speak my truth to you."

Her heartbeat quickened, making her feel half-breathless with anticipation. "So, speak your truth," she said softly. "Tell me why you're here, Brad."

"I'm here because I love you, Simone. I love you more than I've ever loved a woman in my life. I can't imagine my life without you." The words rushed out of him as he took a step closer to her.

"I want to marry you, Simone. I want you to have my babies and I want to build a future with you. I want us to grow old together and…"

He paused as she stepped closer to him and placed her finger over his lips. "Yes," she said, a tremendous joy filling her heart. "Yes, yes," she repeated. "Oh, Brad, I want that, too. I love you,

Brad, and I can't imagine wanting a future with any other man but you."

"Speaking of our future, I have a few cases I need to finish up in DC, but I'm putting in for a transfer to the Chicago department. I'm hoping to be here full-time in the fall. Will that work for you?"

"Of course it will. In fact, I'm going to lighten my fall schedule so I'm not teaching as many classes. I want to have plenty of time to spend with my man. Are you really ready to be in a relationship with a nerdy professor?" she asked.

He laughed. "The sexiest professor I've ever known."

"If that's the case, then kiss me, Brad."

He pulled her into his arms and crashed his lips to hers in a kiss that stole her breath away, shot tingles through her and tasted of the laughter, the mutual respect and support, and the love they would share for the rest of their lives together.

She was vaguely aware of fireworks going off outside, but the fireworks going off in her heart, knowing her future was with Brad, were all she needed to be happy.

* * * * *

*Don't miss a new branch of the Chicago Coltons
in Marie Ferrarella's
Colton 911: Secret Defender,
available next month from
Harlequin Romantic Suspense!*

For a sneak peek, turn the page...

Prologue

If it wasn't for the excruciating pain shooting up and down her leg to the point that it was making tears come to her eyes, Nicole Colton would have been utterly furious with herself.

Of all the stupid things she had done in her life—and there had been at least a number of them over the last fifty-eight years—this definitely took the cake.

She felt like the pathetic embodiment of that awful commercial she had always felt was created for no other reason than to embarrass and humiliate older people—she steadfastly refused to use the term *senior citizen*—and make them feel clumsy and utterly inept. The fact that she was here, sprawled out on the floor after inadvertently taking a slip because of a wet spot, was exceeding aggravating.

Especially since she found that she was unable to pop right back up the way she usually did. The pain was just too excruciating.

The cutting words *I've fallen and can't get up* kept echoing through Nicole's head even as she literally *dragged* herself across the living room floor until she could grasp onto the side of the sofa. She tried to pull herself up but failed. All but completely drenched in sweat from her effort, Nicole paused, panting hard and trying to regroup as she desperately searched for a second wave of strength.

"Okay, Nic, you can do this," she said through clenched teeth, urging herself on even as another sharp wave of pain sliced right through her. "You raised three boys on your own, started your own business, you can certainly get up off the floor on your own."

It wasn't easy.

Several pain-filled minutes later, Nicole finally managed to get herself up to her knees at the sofa cushion. But rather than stand up, all she could do was get herself into a half-lying position and then roll painfully over, all the while biting her lip to keep the cries from emerging and echoing throughout her large house.

Breathing hard, Nicole finally managed to get into a sitting position. When she did, she was all but panting from the exertion.

"Okay, I lied," she said, her face dripping with perspiration. "I *can't* do this."

Instead of going away, the pain was multiplying by leaps and bounds, bordering on unbearable. Although she hated the thought, she had to admit that she had definitely broken something. Moreover, she resigned herself to the fact that she was going to have to call someone and ask for help. Something that went against absolutely every fiber of her being.

But there was no way around it.

Nicole was sweating profusely now. Admitting to weakness was just not in her makeup. She was the one who went out of her way to hold everything together, the one who worked nonstop and still had time to cheer her sons—both her natural-born son, Aaron, and Aaron's two stepbrothers, whom she had taken in when they were barely seven and eight—on in their endeavors.

They were her ex-husband's sons, whom she had taken in when their mother died and her ex decided that they were dragging him down. She treated them like her own and made certain that these "endeavors" they undertook were of their choosing and not hers.

Her catering business had taken off. Things were

finally going so well—and now this, she thought as a new wave of disgust washed over her.

Her head began to spin. The pain was becoming much worse.

She was afraid that if it grew any worse, she was going to wind up babbling incoherently.

Okay, time to get someone here to help her, as much as she hated the idea. Thank heavens she usually kept her cell phone with her. That had more to do with her catering business than anything else, but right now, Nicole was truly grateful that she had slipped her cell phone into her pocket this morning.

Taking a breath to steady herself and to try to keep the pain at bay long enough to make the call, she pressed the keys that would connect her to Aaron's phone.

She definitely wasn't looking forward to this conversation.

Her oldest son ran a couple of gyms and she quite honestly didn't expect him to even hear his phone, much less answer it. But to her surprise, Aaron picked up after the fifth ring.

Just by chance, Aaron Colton was about to make a call when he felt the phone ring in his hand. When he saw the name on the screen, he had a really bad feeling about this.

His mother *never* called him when she knew he was working.

Turning away from the boxing ring, Aaron

blocked out all the other noises in the gym as he answered the call.

"Mom? What's wrong?"

More than anything in the world, Nicole Colton hated admitting to weakness. But the pain was making it really difficult to even breathe now.

Still, she protested, "What…makes…you… think…anything…is…wrong?"

If he hadn't thought there was anything wrong before, he did now. The pain he heard in his mother's voice unnerved him.

He signaled to his assistant to take over as he quickly made his way to the door. "Tell me where you are, Mom. I'm coming to get you," he promised.

Chapter 1

Damon Colton, the youngest of the three Colton brothers, burst into the hospital surgical waiting area. Accustomed to sizing up any area he walked into at lightning speed, he was able to spot Aaron and Nash within seconds. He made a beeline for his brothers.

"How is she?" he asked breathlessly before he had even had a chance to reach them.

"Ornery as ever," Aaron answered.

Feeling stiff, Aaron shifted in his seat. He and Nash had been sitting here on the orange plastic sofa, keeping vigil ever since the ambulance had brought Nicole to the hospital. Although things seemed to be going well, neither brother wanted to step away—just in case.

"I think he's asking about her hip, not the ongoing argument we were having with her about her going to a rehab center once this is all finally behind us," Nash told Aaron.

"Rehab center?" Damon echoed. He hadn't even thought that far ahead. He was just worried about her immediate condition. "Just how bad is Mom?" he asked, looking from one brother to the other. He had gotten no details.

"Not as bad as Aaron is making it sound," Nash told Damon.

It was obvious to them that their undercover DEA agent brother had come here straight from his assignment without bothering to take the time to change out of what he was wearing. Because of his attire and his rather long hair, Damon was getting some very suspicious looks from the security guard. The latter had made it a point to slowly circle the area. For his part, Damon gave the impression of a man on the move who appeared to be less than trustworthy. That was his main intent when he was on the job.

It was all part of the role he was playing.

But role or no role, Damon, like Nash and Aaron, dearly loved the woman who had been mothering and caring for them equally all these years, whether or not they had actually come from her womb.

Aaron took over the narrative. "The short version is that Mom was in a hurry—as she always is—and she slipped on a wet spot on the floor. According to her, she went down hard, and much to her everlasting annoyance, she wound up breaking her hip," he told Damon, repeating verbatim what he had already told Nash when his architect brother had shown up at the hospital shortly after Aaron and their mother had arrived.

Damon, who faced down dangerous drug dealers without batting an eye, physically winced when he heard Aaron's narrative.

"Wow, that really must have hurt. Is she going to be all right?" he asked, looking from one brother to the other for reassurance.

Aaron nodded. "The hip replacement went off without a hitch. No complications," Aaron told him. The relief was all but palpable in his voice.

Damon had been holding his breath the entire way here, not knowing what to think. He'd never been summoned to the hospital because of his mother before. He breathed a sigh of relief now. "Is she awake? Can I see her?" he asked.

Aaron had just waylaid a nurse moments before Damon had arrived, questioning her for an update. "The nurse said that she was still in recovery. We can see her when they finally transfer her to a room," he told his DEA agent brother.

Damon nodded. And then he thought of what

his brother had said to him when he first inquired about their mother's condition.

"You said something about her being ornery," he recalled. "What did you mean by that?"

"When I first got to the house and found her after her fall, it kind of got to me," Aaron admitted. "I guess I lost it and told her she needed to move into a smaller house, not one that was sprawled out on three levels." He flushed. It wasn't his finest hour. "Needless to say, that didn't make her very happy."

"Oh hell, Aaron, you should have known better," Damon told him. "You know how independent Mom is. She has more energy and acts younger than women who are half her age. Saying something like that to her is like rubbing salt into her wounds."

Nash nodded in agreement. "Yeah, you definitely said the wrong thing, brother," he told Aaron, then softened his words. "For all the right reasons," he granted. "But it was still the wrong thing."

Aaron sighed. "I know, I know," he admitted. "But be that as it may, when Mom finally gets to go home, there are going to have to be some changes made—whether she likes them or not." Aaron had always been the decisive one in the family and now was no different than before. "She's going to need a nurse or some live-in help. Maybe both," he added, looking from one brother to the other to see if they understood.

For once, they were all in agreement.

"No argument," Nash told Aaron. "Whatever the cost, we can take care of it."

"You can count me in," Damon said, adding his vote to the others.

"Cost isn't the issue here," Aaron told his brothers. "Whatever it is, it is. The problem, we all know, is getting Mom to agree. You *know* she's going to see this as a restriction."

As if on cue, all three brothers nodded their heads. Their mother was a fighter from the get-go, and knowing her, it was going to be a very steep, uphill battle to get Nicole Colton to loosen her grip on the reins of her life and actually listen to her sons. Even if she knew that their only concern was her safety.

Easier said than done, Aaron thought as he saw the operating room nurse head straight in their direction.

All three brothers rose to their feet in unison as if they were all joined at the hip.

And all three had their fingers crossed as they went to meet the nurse partway.

A single thought was going through their heads. Nicole Colton *had* to be all right. Anything less was just *not* acceptable to the brothers.

"No, no, no," Nicole told her oldest son in no uncertain terms.

It was five days since the accident had happened.

Five days since the emergency hip replacement surgery had taken place. Rather than the standard surgical procedure, she had gotten the more superior "anterior-posterior repair" version. That version of the surgery allowed her to heal faster. But not even her surgeon had expected her to make this much progress, certainly not so quickly, even though she was exceedingly fit, especially for someone her age.

Her surgery had taken place on Wednesday. On Friday she went home and, over all three sons' rather loud objections, Nicole had actually walked up the stairs to her room. She had totally ignored her sons' complaints about her doing too much too soon.

As she crossed the threshold to her bedroom, Nicole felt as if she had just reclaimed a little of her life back. She was *not* about to give that up, not even to placate her sons.

The chorus of noes she had just uttered was in response to yet another attempt on Aaron's part to talk her into having a nurse come and live with her until such time as *they* felt she had recovered.

"Aaron, I don't need a nurse," she informed her son. "I can walk up the stairs. You saw me. If I can do it on the first day I came back, I can do it on the second. And the third," she emphasized. "That means I can take care of myself the way I always have," she proudly concluded. "I don't need someone keeping tabs on me."

Aaron tried again. "Mom, getting someone to

stay here with you isn't an admission of weakness. And it doesn't have to be a nurse," he relented, although he really didn't want to. He felt like a man who was struggling to win at least a portion of the battle before the war was declared officially over. "It can even be a competent paid companion." Although he really would prefer that person to be a nurse. "Think of her as being just a warm, intelligent body who can step in to help you out if the need should come up."

By the expression on her face, he could see he wasn't getting anywhere with his mother, and after spending basically two weeks away from the gyms he ran, Aaron really felt that he needed to get back to work. "Look, Mom, if you refuse to do it for yourself—"

She smiled at that. "Now you get it," Nicole told him happily.

But Aaron wasn't about to be detoured. "Do it for me," he concluded.

Nicole stared at her son in disbelief. "You're not serious."

"Oh, I'm very serious," Aaron assured her. He was accustomed to being listened to without any argument at the gyms he ran as well as with the boxers he trained. This, however, was going to take diplomacy, a gift he hadn't quite developed. He gave it another shot. "Look, Mom, you are very precious to me. To all of us," he stressed. "Now, you had an accident. Granted, we didn't lose you, but we could have if the circumstances had been different.

"Think of this as putting our minds at rest," he told her. "Nash has a job to do, I have a business to run and Damon, well, if Damon doesn't keep his mind clear and focused on his work, it could very well wind up costing him his life." Unwavering, Aaron went in for the "kill."

"You don't want that to happen, do you?"

"Of course not," she cried with feeling. "But," she countered, "I also don't want to become an invalid by just surrendering my independence to set everyone's mind at rest, either. We need a compromise."

Aaron sighed. Determined, he gave it one last try. "Okay, the way I see it, Mom, hiring someone to help you is a compromise."

Nicole met her son's eyes head-on. "Not hiring anyone would be an even better way to go," she pointed out.

"Mom," Aaron said. There was a warning note in his voice. He was reaching the end of his patience. "This is as far as I'm willing to give in. Now until the doctor gives you the 'all clear,' you are going to need someone to be here with you when I can't be and you are going to *have* someone. The way I see it, you can either pick out that someone yourself, or I will do it for you," Aaron said. "Your choice."

Nicole frowned. "I don't really *feel* like I have a choice."

"Trust me, you do," Aaron told her. "Because if you don't make a choice here," he repeated, "I will." Standing over her like this, he knew he was being intimidating—but apparently she needed that. This, he told himself, was for her own good—not to mention his own peace of mind. "So what's it going to be?"

Nicole thought of the young woman she had met and talked with during her first physical therapy sessions at the rehab facility. She had taken an instant liking to Felicia Wagner, a perky, friendly and fresh-faced young woman who was working at the facility part-time.

Nicole smiled as she raised her eyes to her son's. "I think I know a young woman who would be willing to take on the job."

"Ah, finally. Progress," Aaron declared with a sigh. "Why don't you give this lady a call? Whatever she wants to be paid—within reason," he stipulated, not wanting to be taken advantage of, "just say yes. And don't concern yourself with the cost. I'll take care of it."

Nicole shook her head. "You're a good son, Aaron, but I can take care of my own bills."

He dearly loved this woman, but there were times when his mother could be exasperatingly pig-headed. "Mom, everything doesn't have to turn into a tug-of-war. I'm making the request and I'm paying for it. End of discussion," he told her. And then, looking at her face, he added, "Okay?"

A gracious smile rose to his mother's lips as she obligingly nodded her head. In her opinion, she had won. "Okay."

Relieved that this argument had finally been put to bed, Aaron bent over and kissed his mother's forehead. "That's my girl," he said with genuine relief.

He knew how much it had to cost his mother to give in this way. She had always been the last word in independence and for her to agree to have someone come in and stay in the home she considered to be her domain for so many years was a huge deal.

He had to admit that part of him wasn't prepared to win this confrontation so easily. Obviously, playing the "do it for me" card seemed to have really worked wonders, he thought, congratulating himself.

But he wasn't going to overanalyze it. That kind of thing was for working with the fighters who came to him for guidance and training. His analysis kept them alive and moving up the championship ladder. But this was about his mother and he knew better than to be anything but really, really grateful she had stopped fighting him on this and had just agreed to do as he had suggested.

Right now, it was time to get his mind back on running his gyms. The boxers who sought out his particular gyms weren't there because of the showers and the state-of-the-art weight equipment he had stocked. They were there to gain insight into his specific training methods as well as the host of other amenities that he could offer them.

"Do you want me to put in that call for you?" he asked his mother.

As she was already making plans in her mind, her son had managed to lose her. "To who, dear?" Nicole asked, admittedly somewhat confused.

He began to wonder if she had been putting him on after all. "To this person you said you would be willing to have come stay with you until you're ready to be on your own," Aaron explained to his mother, enunciating every word.

Because she loved him, Nicole smiled indulgently. "I still know how to make a phone call, Aaron."

"Then you have her number," he assumed. He knew he was treating his mother like a child and she was going to resent it even if she didn't show it, but he needed to have all this spelled out so he was sure that she was going to do as he asked and not find some way to wiggle out of it.

"Yes, dear, I have her number," she answered patiently. She didn't roll her eyes, but it was there in her voice.

"Good. I can make the arrangements," Aaron offered again.

This time, his mother did roll her eyes. "Aaron, I said I would take care of it. There may come a day when you will have to take care of me," Nicole told her son, "but—much as I appreciate the thought—that day is *not* today."

"Okay, I get that," he allowed, looking at the situation from her point of view. "But I still want to meet this 'caretaker,'" he stressed.

"And you will, dear—once she accepts the job and has gotten accustomed to staying in this 'barn of a house,' as you referred to it in the hospital. But for now, just let me handle this my way."

He wasn't about to back away from this totally. "Will I be meeting her soon?" he asked.

Maybe it was the spill she had taken and the hip fracture that had resulted, but Nicole found that her patience seemed to be in shorter supply than it normally was.

Still, she managed to tell her oldest, "Yes, you will be meeting her soon. Felicia is a very sweet, accommodating young woman, so I'm sure she would be willing to put up with your scrutiny."

Aaron nodded. "Felicia." he repeated, rolling her name over on his tongue. "Pretty name."

"If her name was Maude, would that disqualify her from the position?" Nicole asked, amused.

"No, I just—" Aaron paused, realizing what his mother was doing. "You're yanking my chain, aren't you?"

"With both hands, dear," she answered, flashing a wide smile. "Now, don't you have a life to get back to?" she asked him. "A life that you've been away from much too long?"

"Nothing is more important than you, Mom," he answered honestly.

"I appreciate that, dear," she told him. "But I have taken you away from that gym you worked so hard to get up and running long enough, not to mention the other gyms you're overseeing. Remember, guilt is not helpful for my recovery," Nicole stressed.

"Point taken." There was that independence of hers, rearing its head again. "But I still don't want to leave you alone in the house."

She looked at him, knowing exactly what was going on in his head. "I'm not going to fall again," she informed him.

"I wasn't worried about that," he answered a bit too quickly.

He was lying, she thought. "Yes, you were. You have a tell, Aaron," Nicole said, leaning forward. "When you're not being completely truthful, you get this little furrow in your brow," she told him. She flittered her fingertips across his forehead. "Now, you don't have to stay here and hover over me. If it makes you feel any better, Vita is coming over," she told him.

Vita Yates was her former sister-in-law. The two

women were very much alike, both having weathered divorces from their respective Colton husbands and survived the dealings of a viper-like mother-in-law who could have very easily run a school for unemployed witches in her spare time. The two women had bonded early on and their relationship only grew stronger as the years went by. They also acted as each other's support group, providing encouragement when needed most.

"Aunt Vita?" Aaron asked, surprised. His mother should have told him this to begin with. "You're sure?" he asked, wanting to make sure his mother wasn't just trying to get rid of him.

"Aaron, I broke my hip. I didn't hit my head and get a brain injury. Yes, I am sure. Now go before I show you what a needy, clinging mother can *really* be like."

He made no move to leave. "When is Aunt Vita coming?" he asked.

The doorbell rang just then. "Now," Nicole answered with a smile.

"Okay, you win this one, Mom," he said as he went to answer the door.

"I win them all, dear," Nicole called after her son with a smile.

Aaron sighed. He knew she was right.

WE HOPE YOU ENJOYED
THIS BOOK FROM

HARLEQUIN
ROMANTIC SUSPENSE

Danger. Passion. Drama.

These heart-racing page-turners will keep you guessing to the very end. Experience the thrill of unexpected plot twists and irresistible chemistry.

4 NEW BOOKS AVAILABLE EVERY MONTH!

COMING NEXT MONTH FROM

(H) HARLEQUIN
ROMANTIC SUSPENSE

#2143 COLTON 911: SECRET DEFENDER
Colton 911: Chicago • by Marie Ferrarella

Aaron Colton, a retired boxer, hires Felicia Wagner to care for his ailing mother. Little does he know, the nurse hides a dangerous secret and could disappear at a moment's notice. Does he dare get too involved and ruin the bond building between them?

#2144 RESCUED BY THE COLTON COWBOY
The Coltons of Grave Gulch
by Deborah Fletcher Mello

Soledad de la Vega has witnessed the murder of her best friend. Running from the killer, she takes refuge with Palmer Colton. He's been in love with her for years and doesn't hesitate to protect her—and the infant she rescued.

#2145 TEXAS SHERIFF'S DEADLY MISSION
by Karen Whiddon

When small-town sheriff Rayna Coombs agrees to help a sexy biker named Parker Norton find his friend's missing niece, she never expects to find a serial killer—or a connection with Parker.

#2146 HER UNDERCOVER REFUGE
Shelter of Secrets • by Linda O. Johnston

When former cop Nella Bresdall takes a job at a domestic violence shelter that covers as an animal shelter, she develops a deep attraction to her boss. But when someone targets the facility, they have to face their connection—while not getting killed in the process!

Get 4 FREE REWARDS!

We'll send you 2 FREE Books <u>plus</u> 2 FREE Mystery Gifts.

Harlequin Romantic Suspense books are heart-racing page-turners with unexpected plot twists and irresistible chemistry that will keep you guessing to the very end.

FREE
Value Over
$20

Love Harlequin romance?

DISCOVER.

Be the first to find out about promotions, news and exclusive content!

f Facebook.com/HarlequinBooks

𝕏 Twitter.com/HarlequinBooks

◎ Instagram.com/HarlequinBooks

𝓟 Pinterest.com/HarlequinBooks

You Tube YouTube.com/HarlequinBooks

ReaderService.com

EXPLORE.

Sign up for the Harlequin e-newsletter and download a free book from any series at
TryHarlequin.com

CONNECT.

Join our Harlequin community to share your thoughts and connect with other romance readers!
Facebook.com/groups/HarlequinConnection